ANNA

DIANE BRADFORD

Ark House Press
PO Box 1722, Port Orchard, WA 98366 USA
PO Box 1321, Mona Vale NSW 1660 Australia
PO Box 318 334, West Harbour, Auckland 0661 New Zealand
arkhousepress.com

Cataloguing in Publication Data:
Title: Anna
ISBN: 978-0-6451835-6-6 (pbk)
Subjects: Fiction
Other Authors/Contributors: Bradford, Diane;

Design by initiateagency.com
Cover picture and illustrations by Stuart Bradford

For my Dad, my first and best storyteller.

Huge thanks to Stu for all the wonderful artwork, encouragement and help with editing, and to Annie and Denice for your editing, advice, and enthusiasm!

Contents

Chapter One

Anna

Anna did not know why the birds were still singing in her frightened little village.

No-one else was singing, they were barely talking! She hurried back to her house with her goatskin full of fresh water from the well. There was no lingering today. No chatting to the other children at the well. Everyone was rushing back to their own homes, occasionally nodding a greeting to one another, but mainly scurrying along, eyes down, doing their best to go unnoticed.

Anna's stomach was churning with fear. She would not have left her house that morning given a choice, but they needed water, and if her father came back from a night of drinking and there was no water she would be in trouble! She glanced around nervously but could see no sign of any Roman soldiers. She was terrified of them; only yesterday she had watched them beat a child for getting in their way, and a few days ago she had seen them kill some of her villagers.

As she came near to her house, she looked up and saw her neighbour Mary, beckoning her urgently. Anna began to run, glancing around, looking for any signs of danger.

Mary watched Anna approach, dread gnawing at the pit of her stomach at the news she was about to deliver. Pity filled her as she saw Anna running; she looked so small and vulnerable, her long dark hair flowing behind her in a tangled mess, her brown eyes wide with fear.

As she reached Mary's house, Anna stumbled and fell into Mary's arms who quickly dragged her inside the house.

"Anna, quick! Hide behind here and be quiet, whatever you hear," hissed Mary anxiously, as she pushed her towards the back wall.

Confused and alarmed at the tone of Mary's voice and the look of fear in her eyes, Anna did as she was told and hid behind the large, embroidered blanket that hung from ceiling to floor in Mary's house. Not many people knew that the wall behind the blanket was not entirely flat; there was a small hole about halfway down, just the right size for Anna to hide in. At ten years old, Anna was much shorter than average and very slight, so she curled up into the hole in the wall just as she had done many times before.

Anna was used to hiding behind the blanket; it was a favourite hiding place when Anna played with Mary's grandchildren, although as it was where everyone looked first, it was not highly effective! But just lately it had become a useful refuge when Mary had needed to hide Anna from her own father during one of his drunken rages. He would sometimes take his anger out on Anna and hurt her, but he was always sorry when he sobered up, then he would promise not to drink again and would keep his word for a few days.

This time though, Anna was sure it was something else as she had seen the look in Mary's eyes.

This time, Mary looked scared - really scared!

Mary was not afraid of Anna's father and often stood up to him, so why did she look so frightened? Why did Anna have to hide? If not from her dad, then from who? Was it the Romans? And if so, why wasn't Mary hiding? She held her breath; what was happening?

She was about to ask when she heard voices. Not in Mary's house but in her own house next door. She listened carefully; she could not quite make out what they were saying. They were rough, angry, men's voices - she was not sure if she recognised them.

Maybe they were Roman soldiers! There were plenty of them around – they had turned up a few days ago and shattered the peace in her tranquil little village.

But what were they doing in her house? She listened, holding her breath. She changed her mind; they did not sound quite right for soldiers. They seemed to be throwing things around in her house as if they were searching for something. She winced as she heard one of her clay bowls smash against the wall. She heard their footsteps getting closer, clearly, they were leaving her house and coming towards Mary's!

Anna froze as she heard the men burst through Mary's door without knocking!

Mary was expecting them; they had called earlier looking for Anna and she knew they would be back. She had been frightened by them! They were large, angry-looking men who claimed to know Anna's father. One of them had a hand missing and he had shoved his hand-less arm in Mary's face and spat in anger as he said, "He owes me for this!"

The same man was just as scary this time round when he lunged towards Mary as she backed away, "Where is she, woman? She must be back by now!" the one-handed man yelled, his face red with anger.

"I have no idea what you're talking about and would you mind not coming into my house uninvited!" Mary shouted back angrily, trying to sound brave.

From behind the blanket, Anna could not tell what was happening, but it sounded like they were moving Mary's furniture around. They seemed to be searching Mary's house as well. Anna knew it would not take them long to search Mary's home. She was being generous when she called Mary's home a house. It consisted of only one room; just like her own home that she shared with her father – built from sun-dried mud bricks with a floor made of beaten earth and a slightly raised clay platform at the back where they slept on their straw mattresses.

"You see, whoever you're looking for, she's not here," said Mary.

"We know you're hiding her! Where is she?" one of the men said, sounding threatening. Anna heard Mary gasp!

What were they doing to her? Anna's heart was thumping so hard in her chest she was sure that they would hear her! She clamped her hand over her mouth, convinced that at any moment she would not be able to stop herself from screaming. Suddenly the terrible truth dawned on Anna, and she began to tremble with fear as she realised that she was the one that they were searching for. But why? Who were these men? What did they want from her?

Where was her dad?

"Forget it, she's not here anymore, she must have slipped out the back," said one of the men. "Don't worry, we'll find her," the other one said.

Anna heard footsteps, it seemed like they were leaving.

Anna waited, had they gone? What should she do? She heard the shuffle of feet coming closer.

"Stay where you are until I tell you it's safe," whispered Mary.

It felt like an eternity as she waited, heart pounding, her mind filled with questions, so many questions!

"Ok, love, they're gone, you can come out now. Good job you're so small, not everyone could hide there," said Mary, sitting down on a stool, her hand on her chest, clearly shaken.

Anna squeezed out of her hiding place and rushed over to Mary,

"Mary, are you ok? Did they hurt you? What do they want with me? Who are they?"

Mary grasped Anna's hands with her own rough, wrinkled ones, "Anna, love, sit down and I'll tell you what I know."

Anna sat down and saw Mary's eyes mist over.

Mary began, "I need you to be brave. I'm sorry, I must be quick because it's not safe for you here anymore. From what those men told me earlier, your dad owed them a lot of money and couldn't pay them back. It seems, one of them owed even more money to some slave traders and when he couldn't pay his debt, the slave traders took his hand in part payment!"

Anna winced, who were these horrible men who had dealings with slave traders? How did her dad get mixed up with them?

Mary continued, "He blames your dad, so they came to collect the money he owes. They've searched your house, you know there's nothing of value there, so now they're searching for you."

Anna gasped, "Me? Why me? I have no money! Where's my dad?"

Mary sighed, "I'm sorry, love, I don't know how to say this," she began to cry.

Anna felt her stomach tighten with anxiety, her mouth went dry, "Mary, tell me! What's wrong?"

"Oh Anna, your dad..." Mary shook her head, the tears flowing, barely knowing how to break the news to Anna.

"Mary! You're scaring me!" cried Anna.

"I'm so sorry, love," Mary pulled herself together, "It's your dad, he's... oh dear ... he's been killed, I'm so sorry!" Mary wrapped her arms around Anna and embraced her tightly.

Anna stared wide-eyed, unable to speak, totally shocked.

After a few seconds she found her voice, "Mary... I don't... what happened?... He's what?...

When? How did he? He's dead? But he can't be. No, Mary, I saw him yesterday. No, Mary, he's not!"

"I'm sorry, love," sniffed Mary as she wiped her eyes, "I'm afraid it's true."

Anna just kept shaking her head.

"No, Anna, you must listen!" Mary grasped Anna's shoulders and looked her directly in the eyes.

"He's dead. Very late last night, your dad and some other men got into an argument with some Roman soldiers, it turned violent, and he was killed. I don't know why he was so careless; he can't have forgotten those villagers that were killed a few days ago when the soldiers arrived! He should have left it alone, but you know what he's like and I think he'd been drinking. Anyway, I'm sorry, love, he's gone," Mary gently stroked Anna's cheek and continued, "then these two men turned up, they came earlier when you were out fetching water. I was hoping they'd be gone by the time you came back. When they found out what happened to your dad, they came here looking for you."

"But why do they want me?" asked Anna.

Mary sighed, "Anna, they could get some money for you if they sold you as a slave or gave you to the slave traders to clear their debt."

Anna gasped, and glancing towards the door, she scrambled to her feet, "I have to get out of here!" she screeched. There was no way Anna was going to allow herself to be taken as a slave! Slavery was commonplace, there had been slaves in the trading caravans that had passed through on the way to Jerusalem. She had seen the look on their faces, she had seen the emptiness in their eyes, the hopelessness, and the fear. She had already decided that she would rather die than lose her freedom.

Mary grabbed her by the hand, "Yes you do need to get out of here; but wait! I will help you. Just let me think!"

"Mary, I have to go now! They could be back any moment!"

Mary was flustered, "Hold on. Look, you need to get away from here, not just away from your house but away from the village; if you stay, they'll find you, our village is not large enough for you to hide in for very long!"

Anna was panicking, "Where do I go?"

"If only you had some relatives you could stay with!"

"I know, but there's no-one, it was just me and dad!"

"Ok, wait here, I'm just going to check outside to see if I can see the men." Mary carefully peeped out of her door. Anna crept up behind her and peeked out from behind Mary's dress.

"Anna, stay inside!" hissed Mary, "I can see them!"

Anna caught a glimpse of the men. They were standing talking to someone at the end of the street. Anna realised that she recognised them; she had seen them with her dad on several occasions and had assumed wrongly, that they were his friends. They did not live in the village, but they visited from time to time, and she knew her dad went out drinking with them. Just then, one of the men glanced in their direction.

"Wall now!" said Mary as she pushed Anna back inside, fearful that the men had seen her.

Anna did as she was told and hid behind the blanket once again. Everything felt so unreal, she could not even shed a tear for her dad. She curled up in the hole keeping as still and quiet as possible and closed her eyes somehow hoping this would make her even harder to find.

After a short while, she heard Mary's voice, it was little more than a whisper, "Okay, they didn't see you, they've moved on for now. Stay there, I'm just going to see a friend; I have an idea."

Anna waited, curled up in her hole, behind the blanket. How could everything have changed in such a short space of time? Life had not been perfect, but it was familiar. Up until a few days ago, their village had been a quiet, peaceful place. Located seven miles outside of Jerusalem, it was just a small settlement of houses and tents. Probably no more than a couple of hundred people lived there. It was good farmland; they grew flax, wheat and barley, and up on the hillside were vineyards and fig trees. During the harvest, the whole village came out to help. Anna loved those times, especially the celebrations once the crops had been gathered in.

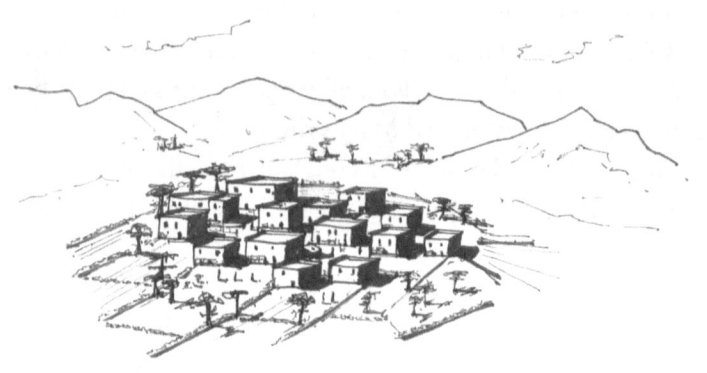

Anna's father, John, had been a carpenter. The only one in the village. He had made a good living especially as Jerusalem was so close and many traders passed through their village. John would regularly go to Jerusalem, joining one of the caravans that came through. It was always safer to travel with a lot of people, the countryside was rife with robbers and highwaymen.

Things had started to go wrong when her dad had injured his hand and was unable to continue with his work. He could no longer earn money doing carpentry so had to try and get a bit of work on the farms which did not pay very well. Anna knew that he was spending far too much of the money he earned on beer, and because of that, there was little money left for food.

Anna considered herself fortunate because they lived next door to Mary who had always looked after her and fed her when her dad could not. Anna loved Mary. She was the one who comforted her and tended to her when she hurt herself. She was the one who taught her how to bake and clean the house; in fact, she did all the things Anna's mother would have done for her had she still been alive. Mary was a grandmother to two children, three if you counted Anna. Actually, Anna spent more time with Mary than Mary's own grandchildren did as they lived quite a distance away in a village the other side of Jerusalem. Anna knew Mary was often cross with her father and disapproved of him. But Anna loved her dad, even though she was a little scared of him. And, as Anna would sometimes say to Mary, "At least I have sandals!" which was more than could be said for some of the poorer folk who could not even afford to buy their children sandals. Life was tough for Anna, but she took comfort in the fact that Mary was always there.

Then just a few days ago the Romans had come! They had been in Jerusalem for many years and had been gradually expanding their influence, taking over the many surrounding towns and villages, easily subduing any resistance they encountered. For some unknown reason they had left Anna's little village alone up until now. The village was very easily taken over with just a small struggle that had resulted in the deaths of five villagers and no Romans.

For the next few days, the villagers tried to live life normally in the presence of the Roman soldiers, but it was very strange and scary especially for the children. Anna was terrified of the soldiers as were most of the villagers, and with good reason; the Roman soldiers could be cruel and harsh and would beat or kill people for the slightest provocation! Anna would lay on her straw mattress at night waiting for her dad to come home from his drinking sessions with his friends. She would often listen out for her dad's footsteps, only to hear the marching of the soldiers' feet disturbing her quiet village. When would they leave?

And now, here she was, hiding not from the Romans, but from men who were in business with slave traders, men she had wrongly thought were her dad's friends. After what felt like hours, Anna heard Mary come back into the house; at least, she hoped it was Mary! She held her breath and let it out again in relief when Mary said, "It's okay, you can come out now."

Anna climbed out of the hole and slipped out from behind the blanket. She gasped in fright as she saw a man standing next to Mary, but when she recognised Zechariah, a man she knew well, she let out a sigh of relief. All the children knew Zechariah, he was a favourite among them because he travelled regularly to Jerusalem with his donkey and cart and would bring back little toys and trinkets that he would sell to them for pennies. Anna had long suspected that Zechariah lost money on this part of his business but made up for it when he sold his goods to the adults.

"It's okay Anna, Zechariah's here to help - he's setting off early tomorrow to go to Jerusalem to the market, and he has agreed to smuggle you out of the village in his cart. He's hoping to meet some friends who live just the other side of Jerusalem. They're a lovely family and he's going to ask them to look after you until we can find something else for you. I know nothing's certain but it's the best we can think of right now. Anna, whatever happens you mustn't come back here! These men will be watching me and your house."

Anna nodded, still in shock, "Mary, I don't want to leave you!" Mary pulled Anna into a hug and wept.

"I need to take her now Mary; those men will be back," said Zechariah.

Zechariah checked outside and after a hasty goodbye, and being careful not to be seen, he took Anna back to his home a few houses away. The men looking for Anna fortunately seemed to have disappeared for the moment.

Zechariah's wife was kind to Anna and tried to persuade her to eat, "You have a long day tomorrow, eat something, you need your strength."

But Anna's mouth was dry with fear, and she barely ate anything.

Anna was given a straw mattress to sleep on that night, she slept fitfully, everything seemed so unreal and so frightening!

A few houses away, Mary also had a sleepless night, thinking now might be the time to leave the village and move in with her son and daughter-in-law. She was in an unusual situation. It was rare for a woman of her age, with family, to live on her own. Most of the dwellings in the village housed large family groups – parents, grandparents, children, sometimes even aunts, uncles and cousins all lived together. But Mary and her husband had stayed in the village when her son and his family had found work the other side of Jerusalem. She had been a widow for a little over a year now. Her husband had left her enough money to stay in her own home, and she was able to make a living doing sewing jobs for the villagers.

Mary's son had been trying to persuade her to move in with them, but she had been reluctant because of Anna. Mary had been there for Anna and for her father ever since Anna's mother had died in childbirth. Mary had cared for Anna like her own child, and this meant John could carry on with his work as a carpenter. Now that John was gone, Mary was all that Anna had and she was seeking desperately for a solution, a way that she could keep Anna with her. Mary suspected that these men were ruthless and would keep on searching for Anna, and she dreaded to think what they would do to the young girl if they found her. Mary agonised over what was best to do for this child that she loved like her own, she knew her son would have taken Anna into his home in an instant, but she had no way of contacting him in time. Mary resigned herself to the harsh reality that she had had no alternative but to send Anna away with Zechariah. She tried not to think about what would happen if Zechariah's friends could not take Anna in. But the situation was desperate, the only thing she knew for sure was that it was not safe for Anna to stay here in the village with her.

Early the next morning while it was still dark, Anna was gently shaken awake by Zechariah's wife and smuggled into Zechariah's little cart. She took one last look at her sleeping village; she could not see much. She thought of her friends asleep on their straw mattresses that she might never see again.

Mary crept out of her house to say goodbye. Silently she hugged Anna, "God be with you, little one," she choked, "keep this over you so no-one can see you." Mary pressed some coins into Anna's hand as she pulled a large hessian sack over her.

Anna whispered a tearful goodbye and put the coins into the pocket that Mary had sewn into her tunic. She sobbed quietly as she wondered if she would ever see Mary again.

Chapter Two

Jerusalem

Anna had a lot of time to think about what lay ahead as she curled up under the hessian sack on a goatskin blanket in the uncomfortable, bumpy cart. As normal, Zechariah was travelling in a caravan of traders on his way to Jerusalem, so she had been told to keep quiet and stay hidden for her own safety. This was easier said than done, the sack was dusty and smelled like old vegetables. She did her best to breathe through her mouth, but she could still smell the musty old hessian and the dust made her want to sneeze. Zechariah had explained to Anna that it would take most of the day to get to Jerusalem, because although it was only seven miles away, the terrain was rough and hilly. Zechariah planned to pitch his tent in Jerusalem with the other traders and whilst there, he would look for the family he knew, who might take Anna into their home. Zechariah would stay in Jerusalem for a few days, and when his business was done would then return to his home.

Zechariah had seen how anxious Anna had become as he explained his plan. "But what if they're not there?" Anna had asked.

"Don't worry Anna, I'm sure we'll meet up with my friends, it's very unusual not to see them when I go to Jerusalem!" Zechariah had tried to reassure her.

But Anna saw a flicker of doubt in his eyes and thought she heard some uncertainty in his voice, and she began to worry even more.

The journey seemed so long to Anna, and it did not help that she could not see anything. Often, she would hear a babble of conversation going on among the travellers, but apart from the times they came close enough to Zechariah to greet him or talk about what they were planning to buy or sell in Jerusalem, she could not make out what they were saying even when she strained her ears to hear.

For some reason Anna's mind went to the day last year when she had met Jesus. Life had been getting more and more difficult with her father.

She had loved her dad and she knew he had loved her in his way, but he had become increasingly distant since the accident that had injured his hand. He had done his best to raise his small daughter after Anna's mother had died during childbirth, but life had not been easy for him. They had muddled along together, and Mary had been a godsend living next door. But life without regular work had taken its toll on her dad and she knew he was drinking a lot of the money he had made doing odd jobs.

On this particular day however, her dad was sober and in a better mood than usual so had suggested that he and Anna take a walk to see if they could find this Jesus that everyone was talking about because it was rumoured that he was nearby. It did not take long for them to find him. Anna was surprised at how easy it was. They asked a few people they met who pointed them in the right direction and in the distance, they saw a crowd.

As they approached, they heard an excited murmuring and saw people straining to see what was going on. Anna pushed her way forwards through the crowds and saw Jesus surrounded by sick people who seemed to be getting healed of their ailments. She was surprised, he looked so ordinary, just like any other man but he was putting his hands on people and they were getting healed! Anna and her dad had been astounded when Jesus put his hands on the eyes of a blind man, and he could see again!

"Can you believe that dad?" Anna asked her father who had managed to squeeze through the crowd to get alongside her.

"I'm not sure. I mean, how do we know he was blind? How do we know he can really see now?"

Jesus kept healing people and when Anna saw a man's withered hand change shape and grow to a normal size in front of her very eyes, she had no more doubts! "Dad!" she tugged at his sleeve, "did you see that? That man's hand actually grew! Right there! It grew! Did you see it dad?"

John had been as astounded as Anna, there was no denying that Jesus had just performed a miracle before their very eyes! They hung around and Jesus started to talk with the crowds. Anna had heard priests talk about God when she had visited a synagogue with her dad on special occasions, but she had never heard anyone talk about God like this.

"It's like he really knows and loves God," she thought.

She squeezed through the crowd to get even closer to Jesus along with some other children. Some of the men that were with Jesus tried to stop them getting too close, but Jesus noticed and told the men off. He beckoned to Anna and the other children.

At that moment Jesus looked at Anna and smiled. Despite all the people crowding around him jostling for his attention, reaching out to him to be healed, he noticed her! In that moment she felt loved, accepted and incredibly happy! She sat with the other children just watching him and listening to him. He laughed with them, played with them, had all the time in the world for them, and she began to have hope that life with her dad would get better.

Anna tried to persuade her dad to ask Jesus to heal his hand, but he just shook his head. She could have stayed with Jesus all day, but some people in the crowd were growing restless as some of the religious leaders began to argue with Jesus. It was the Sabbath, and they said that healing people was against their rules, so Jesus should not be doing it. Anna and her father were taken aback when Jesus called the religious leaders' hypocrites and at this point her dad pulled her away, not wanting to get mixed up with the growing unrest.

"I don't understand, dad, why do some people not like Jesus? Especially the religious leaders and priests, surely they would like Jesus making people better?" Anna asked as they walked hand in hand back to the village.

But her father could not really explain, "I think it's the way he calls God his father. It seems as though he knows God better than they do, and he doesn't appear to worry about all their rules that they seem to think are important; but I'm not sure really. Although, I do agree with Jesus, I've met some religious leaders and priests who really are hypocrites!"

"What do you think though dad? Did you like Jesus? Do you believe him?"

"Well, I'm not sure what I believe, but yes I liked Jesus because he's a carpenter like me!" Her father smiled at her. She loved to remember her dad like that, he was happy and sober, it was the best day!

Anna was brought back to reality with a particularly large bump in the road. She suddenly felt so alone; all she had of Jesus was a memory. It seemed that her new-found hope in Jesus had been misplaced because since that day, life had just got worse, and it was about to become more so. But it helped her to remember Jesus, to distract herself from her current situation. It was his eyes that she remembered the most – they were so penetrating, full of love, laughter, and life. He had held her gaze, not just a passing glance. In that instance it was like he knew her, like they were best friends!

If only she could get to him now, surely he would know how to help her, "God, if you really can hear me, I'd love to meet Jesus again"

Suddenly she had an idea, "That's it! I remember someone in the crowd saying that Jesus had even raised the dead! He brought someone back to life! He could make my dad alive again then everything will be okay, and dad will be happier because he would really believe in Jesus!"

Throwing back the sack, Anna sat up in the cart and called out to Zechariah, "Stop, we have to find Jesus!"

Zechariah pulled his donkey to a stop and wheeled around to face Anna, "Hush, child, get back under the sack!" he whispered urgently. He walked round to the back of the cart and tried to tuck the sack around her. Fortunately, he was near the rear of the group and most people were concentrating on what was ahead, "Just stay still, there are people around!" he whispered as he glanced around furtively. He could not be sure if anyone had seen or heard Anna.

"But I need you to help me find Jesus, he can make my dad alive again, I know he can!" Anna said, struggling to stop Zechariah pulling the sack over her.

"I wish he could, Anna, but your dad has already been buried. Now lie still, I will tell you when it's safe to come out - not long now."

And for the first time, Anna wept for her father, and then for herself. The only thing she was sure of was that she did not want to end up in the hands of slave traders! What if Zechariah's friends could not take her in? What if they sold her into slavery?

An hour and a half later, Anna began to hear more voices and the cart slowed but did not stop as Zechariah guided his donkey through one of the gates leading into Jerusalem. She heard Zechariah greet a few people but waited quietly until he pulled back the sack and helped her out of the cart.

Anna looked around. She had never seen so many buildings! Some of them were two or three times the height of her house! Maybe even more!

Zechariah had stopped in an alleyway behind some houses. He had found a relatively quiet place to allow her to climb out of the cart discreetly without being noticed, "Here, stretch your legs for a bit and then you can get back in the cart while I go and see if I can find my friends – I normally meet them not far from here."

After a short time, after Anna had walked around for a while, Zechariah told her to get back into the cart, "I won't be long," he said as he tucked her under the sack, "stay here and don't make a sound."

"What if you can't find them or they can't take me?" worried Anna.

"Then we'll think of something else. Don't worry, now stay still and be as quiet as you can!" replied Zechariah, as he walked away into another street.

Once again Anna had heard the uncertainty in his voice and seen that same doubt flicker in his eyes; that was enough to cause her to panic! Her mind in turmoil, Anna grabbed the blanket she had been curled up on and ran! She was terrified of Zechariah being unable to find his friends and him having to take her back to the village where the slave traders would find her. She had heard that there were thousands of people living in Jerusalem, maybe if she tried to blend in with the crowds, no-one would notice her, and she would be safe.

When Zechariah returned to the empty cart, he knew it was pointless to look for Anna. He had been gone for at least half an hour; she could be anywhere by now. He had searched high and low for his friends but to no avail. What was he going to tell Mary? That was not a conversation he was looking forward to! He sighed, "God, please look after her," he prayed.

Anna had weaved her way through some alleyways and stumbled upon a bazaar. She had heard about these from her dad. They had a few market stalls in her village, but they were nothing like this! There were so many of them! She began to wander through the stalls in a complete daze. She was mesmerized by the huge number of people – and the noise! So much talking, yelling, laughing! A lot noisier than her own little village. People seemed in more of a rush here, she narrowly avoided being bumped into several times.

"Can you people not see me?" she muttered to herself angrily when she had to step out of the way as someone almost backed into her, "Although, that might not be a bad thing!" she concluded, as her purpose for being in Jerusalem was to go unnoticed.

By now it was late afternoon. For just a few moments she forgot her own predicament as she looked at the stalls where people were selling all kinds of fabrics, leather, blankets made of goatskin and wool, then others selling ointments and perfumes of many kinds. Then there were the food stalls; bread, meat, fish, and fruit – different varieties of fruit, some that she had never seen before. Anna breathed in the unfamiliar smells. It felt hot in Jerusalem, warmer than her village, the air was not as fresh.

She stood wide-eyed. Her father had visited Jerusalem many times when he took some of the wooden toys he had made to sell at the market, but he had never taken her with him, she had always stayed with Mary.

Anna fingered the coins in her pocket. She so wanted to buy something, but then she thought better of it; luxuries were for rich people, she needed to save her money for food.

Anna wandered on; her stomach rumbling with hunger, she began to feel weary and started to think about going home.

With a start she realised that she had no home in Jerusalem! Nowhere to sleep! She had just come to a tentmaker's stall who was closing for the day, when she remembered with a pang that her father used to own a tent which he slept in when he came to Jerusalem, "I wonder what happened to it?" she thought, "I should have looked for it, I could have slept in it!"

Panicking now and only just keeping herself together, she wandered around, not knowing what to do. She started to look for somewhere to spend the night. The dark was beginning to descend, and she was feeling incredibly alone and frightened. She began to wish she had stayed with Zechariah, but even if he was still in the same place, she had no idea how to get back there.

"I just need to find somewhere out of the way where no-one will see me," she said to herself.

Jerusalem was crowded with buildings, dwellings of every description, large and small. The streets were uneven, narrow, winding but also wide and straight in places. There were so many alleyways, some leading to other alleyways, some to wide streets, some to large squares, and some were just dead ends. It was all so bewildering to a small girl from a small village! Anna found an alleyway just like the one Zechariah had first stopped his cart in. It seemed quiet, so she found a corner and curled up on the dusty ground in between a couple of old baskets that someone had left lying around. She tucked the blanket around herself and tried to get to sleep - which was hard to do because Jerusalem did not want to sleep as early as she did. She slept on and off out of sheer exhaustion and dreamed of her comfy straw mattress back home.

The next morning, Anna woke early while it was still dark; she did not know where she was for a moment, but then it all came flooding back to her, the despair felt like a crushing weight on her chest. What was she to do? She stretched out and listened hard – were there any people around? She could not hear anything other than a dog barking in the distance, so she decided to stay where she was and try and come up with a plan.

But all she could think of was home. She thought about all the times she had complained about getting up and having to start her day by fetching water – if only they had lived closer to the well!

She remembered drawing water from the well and carrying it back home in the goatskin. Then she would make some bread with the flour she had ground down from the barley seeds she had bought the day before. She would miss baking bread in Mary's clay oven. It was Mary who had taught her how to grind down the barley seeds and make the bread. They used to laugh together as they imagined being rich enough to make bread out of wheat-flour. She wondered if she would ever taste such food.

Anna was startled from her daydream by being roughly shaken, "You can't stay here," said a gruff voice, "clear off!"

Anna gasped in fear and ran as fast as she could. She stopped when she could run no more and bent double trying to catch her breath while checking that she was not being followed.

Shaken, Anna began to explore her surroundings, clinging nervously to the sides of the buildings trying not to be noticed, "My blanket! I left my blanket!" she scolded herself for being so careless. She would have to go back and see if it was still where she had left it. She realised very quickly that she had no idea how to get back, "It all looks the same to me," Anna thought helplessly.

Anna realised that it was easy to get lost, although you could only get lost if you had somewhere you needed to be, and she did not! She climbed up and down steps, in and out of narrow passageways and eventually, without knowing how, stumbled upon the bazaar that she had seen the day before. She found some steps overlooking the bazaar and sat halfway up them not knowing what to do. The day was yet to begin for many people, so it was still relatively quiet.

As the sun rose, so the city came to life. The stalls at the bazaar near the city gates were being set up once again. Anna climbed down the steps and wandered past a bread stall, her stomach rumbling. Should she buy any food? How long would her money last? Should she wait until she was really hungry? She was not used to having any money of her own; what if someone saw that she had money and took it from her? Then she would have nothing. Feeling unsure and fearful, Anna moved on.

She wandered through the bazaar, pausing at a stall that sold different fabrics and tunics. Without thinking, she touched the material and ran her fingers over the fine embroidery. Sadly, she remembered that Mary was going to teach her how to embroider so that when she was older, she could wear a longer tunic that she had embroidered herself. It was a mark of growing up; when girls were young, they wore short tunics, then as they grew up and became women, they would get to wear longer tunics and if they were clever enough, they could embroider them to make them look pretty.

Suddenly, she was shaken out of her thoughts when the stallholder came up to her and slapped her hand away, "Don't touch with your filthy little hands!" he yelled.

Once again Anna ran, dodging through the steadily building crowds until she could neither see nor hear the angry stall holder. She rubbed her stinging hand that was now red as well as being grubby and decided to find some water to drink and wash her hands in. She realised that she must already look scruffy and dirty, like some of the other children she had seen running around.

She trudged wearily for a while, becoming increasingly thirsty, not daring to ask anyone where the nearest water was. After about half an hour she found a well; there was a bucket tied to a rope for people to use to draw the water out, but Anna realised she had no goatskin to keep the water in.

"Here you are, my sweet, borrow my goatskin, get yourself a drink," said a kind voice.

Anna looked up at the kind lady and took the goat skin from her.

"Thank you," she whispered as she lowered the bucket, drew out some water, poured it into the goatskin and took a long cool drink. The lady smiled; she had friendly eyes and reminded her of Mary, and, for one small moment, Anna wanted to fling herself into her arms and cry and be comforted and looked after. Anna turned away to hide her watering eyes and, breathing deeply, she got her emotions back under control. As she turned back, the woman had gone, completely disappeared! Anna looked for her but there were quite a few people milling about and she was nowhere to be seen. Anna held onto the goatskin and, going against everything she knew to be right, she got up and ran before the lady remembered she had left it.

Chapter Three

Isaac

When Anna stopped running, she found herself near a bread stall. Her stomach rumbled with hunger. She wondered whether now was the time to buy some bread to eat. As she pondered, she saw a young boy, who looked just a little bit older than herself, and watched with interest as he weaved in and out of the crowds. He looked like he was asking people for money or food as he kept going up to them holding out his hands. She wondered if he was an orphan like herself. He was barefoot and looked scruffy, dressed in a tunic that looked as though it might have fitted once but was now too big for his skinny frame.

"I expect he's as hungry as I am," Anna thought, "probably even more than I am."

Anna kept watching as a lady gave the boy some money. He immediately came up to the bread stall near Anna and bought some bread which he ate hungrily. Anna began to panic; would she have to beg like that boy? Would she have the courage to beg? She had some money for now, but how long would it last? What if no-one gave her anything? Desperately trying to hold herself together, Anna hurried away from the bazaar. She was so hungry, but so afraid of spending her money in case it ran out. What should she do? She found a corner in an alleyway to sit in and hugged her knees, rocking backwards and forwards in distress, "What do I do? What do I do?" she asked herself over and over, then she spoke sternly to herself, "Come on, pull yourself together, you'll have to get tougher if you want to stay alive!"

In the end, Anna was so hungry, she went back to the bread stall and bought some bread with a few of the coins that she had.

She tucked into the bread eagerly and only after she had eaten all of it, did she think about saving some for later, "Okay, great, so now I only have enough money left for a few days, and I should have saved some bread for tomorrow!" she chided herself.

Living on the streets was not going to be easy. Panic started to rise again, "I can't do this!" she despaired, tears starting to flow leaving trails down her grubby cheeks.

Anna had never felt such hopelessness and fear. Not even knowing what the next few hours held was terrifying! Where would she sleep tonight? She could not go back to that alleyway she slept in last night even if she could find it, because that man might be there to chase her away again.

"God, if you can hear me, I need help," she sobbed.

Anna was a Jew. Her father had taught her a little about God. She had learnt a bit more at the synagogue. She did not understand much of what she had heard, she knew there were right and wrong things to do, and it was important to be good if you wanted to please God, but at the same time, there were so many rules to follow that it seemed impossible to please God . Her dad had never been able to help her with her questions, so many questions! "Anna, we are simple folk, leave the questions to the priests and scholars," he had said. He had told her stories about their Jewish history, about Abraham and Moses and she had listened, fascinated.

She knew God had a history of rescuing his people; but did that include her? God probably could not even hear her, or even know about the trouble she was in! Then she remembered Jesus, and the way he had spoken about God. It was totally different to anything she had ever heard. Jesus clearly really loved God and had seemed to speak about God as if he cared for people like her.

"Oh Jesus, I don't really know you, or if you were telling the truth, but I need help!" she cried in desperation. Then she thought how ridiculous she was being, how could Jesus even hear her? Although, there was something special about him and it seemed to help her calm down when she talked to him, even if she couldn't see him.

Anna spent the rest of the day wandering around the city, desperately trying not to be noticed. Every time someone looked at her, she turned away, worried that they might recognise her.

She knew that if her father's "friends" saw her they would probably know who she was because they had seen her with her dad on several occasions. She had no idea where they lived; what if they came from Jerusalem or even travelled here? They might well be in Jerusalem right now as she knew they did not live in her village, so they had probably not stayed there for long. And what if there were other slave traders looking for stray children? She knew that the men that were after her were not the only slave traders around. Some people voluntarily sold themselves into slavery because they were so poor and could not feed themselves, and it was the only way to stay alive; she knew too that some of the slave traders were ruthless and kidnapped people off the streets. She had to make sure that did not happen to her!

Anna felt as though she stood out in the crowd - of course she did not, people barely noticed her, but she was so frightened, she felt as though everyone was watching her. Other people seemed to have a purpose, friends to talk to, lives to get on with, but she had nothing to do but wander around and try and stay invisible.

Tired of walking, Anna climbed up some rickety old steps and sat at the top, watching the people in the bazaar. The sun was hot, and she had nowhere else to go. With a good view of the bazaar, Anna amused herself by making up stories about the people she could see; it was a useful distraction from her fears.

Anna was hungry again, her stomach began to rumble, but she resisted the temptation to buy any more food. As the day drew to a close, Anna needed to find somewhere to spend the night. She knew she could not stay on the steps where she was now sitting, so she made her way back down towards the bazaar. The stallholders were packing up for the night, she assumed many of them were going home to their families, but some gathered together near the city gate. She wondered why so many people were still around. Then she noticed that they were grouped near an old man who appeared to be telling a story.

She moved a little closer and found somewhere to sit so that she could hear. The old man was telling the story of Joseph. Anna listened, fascinated; it was not the first time she had heard this story, but she knew it was an important part of her Jewish history. This old man was a good storyteller! She listened, transfixed, and for a moment, in her imagination was transported back in time to Egypt with Joseph as he was sold as a slave to Potiphar. She listened as the storyteller told how Joseph prospered until he was falsely accused and thrown into prison.

"Joseph even thrived in prison," the storyteller continued, "the guards realised that they could trust him and soon put him in charge of all the other prisoners. One day two new prisoners arrived; they had come directly from Pharaoh's palace. One was his cupbearer, the other his baker. They had displeased Pharaoh in some way."

"Probably spilt the wine and burnt the bread!" someone interrupted, as the other people including the storyteller laughed.

As the laughter died down, the old man continued, and people were once again paying attention. Anna enjoyed the familiar story; of Joseph's rescue from prison, and his interpretation of Pharoah's dreams that resulted in Egypt and ultimately his own people, the Israelites, being saved from famine. "…and so, God in his wisdom preserved the tribes of Israel, our ancestors," finished the storyteller.

Anna was as disappointed as everyone else when the story ended; it had been a wonderful if only temporary distraction from her predicament. But as the listeners drifted away, she felt the familiar panic rising as she thought about where she was going to sleep. Wiping away the tears that were starting to form in her eyes, Anna tried to calm herself down, "Joseph must have been frightened too when his brothers sold him as a slave," she told herself, "but he kept trusting God. I need to try and be brave like Joseph!"

Anna walked slowly back to the now empty bazaar.

"Could I hide under these tables to sleep?" she thought as she came across a stall that had sheets of material hanging down all the way to the ground.

Anna wondered why the stallholder had left the sheets on the table when he packed up for the night. She looked around to make sure no-one was watching and carefully lifted the corner of the nearest sheet to see what was underneath. Strewn about under the stall were baskets of various shapes and sizes. A perfect hiding place!

Anna glanced around again and slipped underneath the table. Fortunately, being small for her age had its advantages, and so she managed to squeeze herself in between a couple of baskets.

She did not sleep well that night, the ground was hard, it was very cold and without her blanket she soon started shivering. In addition to this, she was terrified of being discovered.

Anna was awake well before the stallholder arrived the next morning. She scrambled out from under the table, almost forgetting to pick up her goatskin, but, remembering at the last moment, she grabbed it and ran. Not that there was anyone nearby to see her, but she was not taking any chances!

After visiting the well to re-fill her goatskin, Anna went back to the bazaar which by now was bustling with activity. She took some of the coins out of her pocket, and deciding that she needed to eat, she bought some bread.

Anna made her way back up to the same steps she had found the day before and sat there watching people shopping and bartering with the stall holders. She looked at the bread in her hand and broke it in half and half again, deciding to eat one piece now and save the rest for later. As she watched the people in the bazaar, the men who were after her came back to her mind, surely, she hoped, she would be hard to find in Jerusalem, there were so many people! She remembered her dad telling her once that thousands of people lived in the city.

She wondered, not for the first time, if the men would even bother to keep looking for her and would they give up their search if they could not find her in her village? Every time she thought she saw someone looking in her direction, she started, ready to run if she needed to.

The sun was high in the sky and the shadows were short, so it was not just her stomach that was telling her it was lunch time. She rubbed her tummy as she thought about eating some more bread, "No!" she scolded herself, "you need to save it for this evening and the next day!"

But by mid-afternoon, she had given in and eaten another piece of the bread, trying to ignore how quickly her supply of food and money was disappearing. What would she do in a couple of days when her money ran out?

She stayed on the steps for the rest of the afternoon.

Suddenly, she spotted the same boy whom she had seen the day before begging for money. She recognised his stained tunic, with the bundle of cloth tied around his waist and tousled light brown hair that came down to his shoulders. This time he was buying some apples, clearly, he had already been successful with his begging today.

As Anna followed him with her eyes, he turned and looked up at her as if he knew she was watching. Embarrassed, Anna averted her gaze and pretended to be busy with something on her tunic.

Isaac looked up at the small girl sitting at the top of the steps; he had spotted her yesterday wandering aimlessly. She had caught his attention because she reminded him of a girl that he had once witnessed being captured by slave traders. It was a memory that still haunted him. At that time, he had stood by and watched; he had been too afraid to do anything to help her, because the girl's captors had been far too big and strong. He knew in his heart that there was nothing he could have done, but there was still a niggling doubt in the back of his mind that made him wonder if he should have tried to save her. He had made a vow that if he was ever in a similar situation again, he would do his absolute best to help. The girl sitting at the top of the steps even looked the same, she was small and skinny and had long thick brown hair that could have been pretty if it were not so knotted. As he bit into his apple, he wondered what this girl's story was. He had noticed the despair on her face, the way she jumped at the slightest noise; he assumed she was an orphan like himself, running away from something or someone, trying to survive each day – she certainly looked like she had no-one to care for her. He was sure she was newer to this life than he was. Isaac suddenly felt protective towards this unknown girl. He decided to go and talk to her.

Isaac knew what it felt like to be scared and alone. He remembered the day that he had been forced out on the street by the people who had taken him in after his mother left him.

A lump came to his throat as he remembered his mother. She was so kind and gentle to everyone and devoted to Isaac. She had done her best to provide for him by making and repairing clothes for people. She had taken herself out of the city when she contracted leprosy before she was forced out by the priests to live in the caves with the other lepers. Their neighbours had grudgingly taken him in, but he was not a welcome addition to their family as they already had too many mouths to feed. He had not been allowed to go and see his mother; they would not let him visit her for fear of his catching leprosy and bringing it back to the house. Then one day they informed him that his mother had died, and as he was not contributing to his upkeep and he ate so much, he could either leave and take his chances on the street or they could sell him to the slave traders.

Isaac did not even need to think about it. He left. Very quickly in case they changed their minds and decided to try and get some money for him. Even now, he was very wary of being caught by slave traders.

Life had taken on a predictable pattern. During the day he begged for money or food, and every night he slept somewhere different, amongst boxes, old sacks, or in ruined buildings.

He had stolen bread a couple of times, but it was a risky business as the punishment, if he got caught was very severe and he did not want to lose a hand!

Isaac began to make his way to where Anna was sitting on the steps, "Hi," he said as he approached her.

Anna lifted her eyes from her tunic and looked down at Isaac, she had noticed him heading in her direction but had decided not to run away as he seemed to pose no threat.

"Hi," Anna replied in a croaky voice as she realised it was the first word she had uttered aloud that day.

"Want an apple?" asked Isaac.

Normally Anna would not take food from strangers, but she was hungry, and knowing that he had bought more than one apple, she said, "Yes please."

Isaac sat himself down next to Anna, untying what turned out to be an old travel cloak from around his waist.

They munched quietly on their apples for a while, then Isaac turned to her and introduced himself, "I'm Isaac by the way, what's your name?"

"Anna," she whispered.

"Hi Anna, I've seen you around a few times today. I think I saw you buying bread earlier?"

"You did, and I've used most of my money now!" Anna instantly regretted saying she had any money left at all. What if he tried to take it?

Isaac noticed the guarded look in her eyes and made no comment, "Where's your home? Have you got any parents?"

It was not long before they were swapping stories, Isaac explaining that he was an orphan trying to survive and Anna explaining that she too was an orphan and on the run from ruthless slave traders.

"So, where are you sleeping tonight?" asked Isaac.

"I don't know," Anna replied wiping away a tear, trying not to show that she was afraid.

"I could show you some places I've found," said Isaac, "do you want to come and see them?"

Anna was wary of trusting this young boy, but she noticed that Isaac had kind eyes and he had at least shared his food with her. Could she trust him? She felt she had little choice, she would soon run out of money and was not confident she could beg, and she certainly did not know the best places to sleep; she needed a friend if she was to survive!

"Ok," she shrugged trying to sound more confident than she felt. "The sun's going down, we should go," said Isaac jumping to his feet. Surprisingly, Isaac led her to the city gates.

"We're not leaving the city, are we?" worried Anna. "It's not safe outside the gates!"

"It's not safe inside the city either! Don't worry, I've been here loads of times!" Isaac replied. They walked through the gates and climbed up the hillside, past some olive groves.

"Where are we going?" asked Anna.

"There's an old derelict barn up here, not much of a roof but it gives a bit of shelter."

The air felt a little fresher as they climbed the hillside. The ground was uneven, and Anna stumbled a few times.

Anna felt safer once they were in the barn. It was beginning to get dark, even though the moon was bright. Anna looked out over Jerusalem and gazed wistfully at the houses with lamps lit, imagining families sitting together, eating meals, the young children already in bed. She sighed and turned her attention to the place she was spending the night.

"You sometimes get goats in here," Isaac explained as he kicked some droppings away with his bare feet. Anna nodded with a small smile, spending the night with goats was something she was used to, and it seemed that Isaac was too. It was commonplace for poorer folk to share their one-roomed houses with their goats in the winter. Isaac chuckled, "I guess, like me, you're used to it!"

The barn itself was made of stone, it looked like it had been quite a bit bigger at some point but all that was left was a small corner that someone had propped up some bits of wood against to make a shelter. There was at least part of the original roof left with a few holes in, but all in all, Anna thought it was quite luxurious compared to sleeping amongst some old baskets or under a table. The ground was hard but dry and there was some old but relatively clean straw in the corner.

"Here, you have my cloak," said Isaac, "and I'll sleep on the straw."

"Thank you," replied Anna, grateful for some warmth. She did not know if she would be able to sleep sharing the barn with a boy she hardly knew, but, both she and Isaac were so exhausted they fell asleep within minutes and slept through until morning.

They both woke up feeling refreshed. Anna was again disorientated at first, but then everything all came flooding back and the fear that had locked itself away in her dreams clawed its way back to the forefront of her mind.

"Sleep well?" yawned Isaac, stretching.

Anna nodded; not even sure she could speak as her throat had suddenly gone dry with fear. "It's okay, it will get better," Isaac seemed to understand how she felt.

Anna began to sob. Now Isaac was scared! Dealing with a crying girl was not something he was used to! "It's going to be alright," he patted her shoulder awkwardly, knowing full well that he could make no such guarantee. Isaac survived by not thinking too much about the days to come. If he thought about how everything was going to work out, he would quickly become overwhelmed by his circumstances. Much to Isaac's relief, Anna began to get herself back under control.

"Sorry," she whispered.

"It's okay, it's alright to be scared. I was at first, still am sometimes, and I guess you miss your dad; It's only been a few days for you. My mum died a few months ago, so I suppose I've got used to it a bit more."

"What happened to your dad? You didn't mention him yesterday," Anna said.

Isaac shrugged, "Nothing to talk about really; he died when I was a baby. Mum never really talked about him. We lived with my grandparents for a while until they died. Why does everybody have to die?" Isaac tried to make light of it.

Anna sighed, "I don't know, I just don't know what's going to happen to me!"

"Look, I don't know what's going to happen to me either, but why don't we just stick together? Then we can help each other." Isaac felt increasingly protective towards this girl; maybe if he could keep her safe, it would make him feel better about not being able to save that other little girl from the slave traders.

He stood up and formally held out his hand, "Hello, my name is Isaac, I'm 13 and I'm your friend, and I promise I will stick with you and look after you." he said trying to keep a straight face.

Anna stood up too, wiped her eyes and giggled. Shaking Isaac's hand, she said, "Hello, I'm Anna, I'm 10 and I'll let you be my friend and I promise I will stick with you, and I will look after you!"

"No, I'll look after you, I am the oldest and a boy!"

"No, I'll look after you, cos I'm a girl and cleverer than you!" Anna stuck her chin out defiantly, which made Isaac smile.

"Ok, how about we look out for each other, but I'm in charge cos you're so small?" he laughed.

Formalities over, they decided to go back down the hill to try and find some food. The gates opened early so there was no problem getting back inside the city. The two children joined themselves onto a caravan of traders just arriving to set up their stalls; Isaac had explained to Anna that it was always better to try and go unnoticed when leaving and entering the city.

Jerusalem was still waking up, so the stalls were not yet open for business.

"Follow me," said Isaac, "there's a baker on the outskirts of the city who makes the best bread, and he starts baking really early. But he hates children so you mustn't let him see you, and his wife's just as bad – she's a miserable old woman!"

They walked quickly through the streets, Anna feeling nervous. She started to think she might be able to find the bakery on her own just by following her nose. The delicious smell of baking bread grew increasingly strong and made her stomach rumble loudly.

As they drew closer to the bakery, Isaac took Anna's hand and put his finger to his lips, "Shhh!". They sidled up to the door and waited nervously.

Chapter Four

Angry Eyes

The bakery was the biggest Anna had ever seen. It looked like it was attached to a large two storey house on one side and a barn on the other side. Anna decided that the people who owned the bakery must be incredibly rich! Her own one-roomed house was half the size of the bakery alone! She could hear goats bleating from the barn, "I guess they don't have to share their house with their goats!" she thought.

The baker, Simeon, and his wife Lydia lived in the house alone and owned the adjoining bakery and barn with the goats. They made a good living selling bread and goats' milk to market traders and individual customers. People would happily go out of their way to buy Simeon's baked goods. He made the best bread and cakes in Jerusalem; at least that was the popular opinion!

Simeon was a large man, with big, tanned muscular arms, and dark curly hair. He had his back to the children and was putting a tray of fresh-baked bread on a table to cool near the door of the bakery which was open to let the heat out into the street, which quite frankly felt just as hot by midday.

"When he goes to the oven to get more bread, that's when we sneak in and take some. He won't see us because he will still have his back to us, so it will be easy," instructed Isaac in a whisper.

"Hold on Isaac, what do you mean? What will be easy? We can't just take the bread! That's stealing! You can't steal Isaac! What if you're caught? Do you want to lose your hand?" hissed Anna.

"It's okay Anna, trust me, I won't get caught! This is one of the only places I steal from. I wouldn't steal from the bazaar - well except for one place - it's too dangerous. But this is easy! There's no-one around, we won't be seen, and even if we are, this guy is too slow to catch us!"

Anna was petrified, but they needed to eat, and she only had a few coins left. She wrestled with her conscience too. Mary had taught her that it was wrong to steal, but Mary had not imagined that Anna would ever be in this situation. Before she could stop him, Isaac was creeping through the bakery door and Anna held her breath as he went inside.

Anna's eyes were fixed on the large baker who had his back to Isaac. She silently willed him not to turn around. Careful to be as quiet as he could, Isaac swiftly picked up a piece of flatbread and backed out slowly watching the baker to make sure he was not seen. Anna was rooted to the spot in fear and did not get out of the way in time when Isaac backed out of the doorway and trod on her foot causing her to gasp in pain!

Simeon spun around!

Anna froze in fear as she locked eyes with the fierce looking baker. Simeon's face contorted to anger in an instant, his brown eyes dark and menacing. For one bizarre moment Anna fleetingly compared his eyes to the eyes of Jesus – they could not have been more different!

Isaac grabbed Anna's hand and pulled her away just as Simeon roared at them and tried to grab them!

They ran as fast as they could, not stopping until they found an alleyway where they could catch their breath. Heart pounding, Anna apologised, "I'm sorry, I should have got out of your way, we would have been okay! He was so scary!"

"Doesn't matter," said Isaac lightly, "we have some bread, and all our hands are still attached!"

Anna was shaking with fear, it took her some time to calm down, "We can't do that again Isaac! Promise me please!"

Isaac looked at her strangely, knowing that he could promise no such thing. He was tempted to lie to her but decided that Anna needed to grasp the harsh reality of living on the streets, "I can't promise that Anna. We must eat. But I do promise that I will always be as careful as I can."

Anna calmed down and they both ate the bread hungrily.

"What's the matter?" asked Lydia, as she came downstairs and found her husband muttering angrily to himself.

"Street kids! Stealing my bread again. I nearly had one of them this time!" spat Simeon. He would have loved to have given those children a beating, stealing from him! He worked hard, how dare they!

Lydia shrugged resignedly and turned to pick up a goatskin to go and fetch some water. Simeon stopped kneading his dough and watched his wife leave, her thin back a little stooped; she was such a changed person from the carefree woman that he had married. His mind went back to when they had first met; Lydia, so young and full of life, her eyes sparkling, her thick brown hair neatly braided. She had taken pride in her appearance, wearing the beautiful tunics that she had skilfully made and embroidered herself. He had loved her confidence, there had been almost an air of mischievous fun about her. Although it had been an arranged marriage, Simeon and Lydia considered themselves to be extremely fortunate because they had, over time, fallen in love with one another.

Life had been sweet for them up to a point. Simeon was a skilled baker, something he had learnt from his own mother, much to the disgust of his father who had wanted him to follow in his footsteps and go into the priesthood. However, Simeon was adamant that he wanted to become a baker despite his father's disapproval. He had begun to work for a baker and did so well that he soon got enough money together to open his own bakery.

He and Lydia had been so excited, and his father had grudgingly agreed that perhaps he was doing the right thing. Simeon had become more and more successful, and when his parents had died, he had inherited a small fortune. They were quite rich and did not need to work anymore, but Simeon loved his baking and had become obsessed with making as much money as possible. Only one thing had spoilt it. They had not been able to have any children. Try as they might, it had just not happened for them. Over time they had both become more and more bitter and had grown to resent people who had children - especially those who had a whole brood of them! This meant that as their friends began to have children, they could not bear to be with them, so they had cut themselves off from people and had fewer and fewer friends.

Life had become a drudgery; the only thing Simeon enjoyed was his baking and it hurt him to watch his wife wallowing in pain and becoming more withdrawn as time went on. He felt angry and frustrated that he could do nothing about it. They had even stopped going to temple as they both started blaming God for not giving them children.

"Children are meant to be a gift from God," Lydia had said, "so what's wrong with us? Why won't he give us children?"

Simeon growled in frustration, his anger which was always simmering just below the surface, reared its head at the stolen bread and he wanted to take it out on those two children. If they tried to steal from him again, he would make sure they were very sorry indeed!

Lydia was deep in thought as she went to fetch the water from the well. She understood why Simeon was so angry, she just wished he would not take it out on the children. She felt sorry for them. They were probably hungry, maybe they did not have a family.

She was aware that being childless had drained her of her joy and she knew that she herself had become more and more bitter and angry. It had got to the stage where she and Simeon would not talk about it anymore, in fact, they talked less and less about anything. Their life together had started with such promise, was this it then for the rest of their days? Lydia felt a huge wave of depression wash over her and she angrily wiped away the tears as she walked and did what she always did; locked away her pain and got on with her day.

"You just need practise; all you have to do is walk up to people and ask for money or food. Tell them you're an orphan, tell them you're hungry, always say please and thank you. Look for women who have children, they're more sympathetic. They are much more likely to give you money. And just remember, the very wealthy are often not as generous as the poorer people." Isaac was giving Anna advice on how to beg effectively as they made their way towards the bazaar.

"But what if they get angry with me, or shout at me?"

"Just walk away, no harm done."

Anna was not so sure.

"Look, just stick with me, we'll beg together. You don't have to say anything, just stay by my side and try to look hungry," said Isaac.

"I am hungry!" grumbled Anna.

"Then it won't be a problem, will it?" laughed Isaac.

"Okay I'll try. I guess it's the only way to get food. I suppose we'd better save my little bit of money for the times we can't get any money from begging. And we won't be able to visit 'Angry Eyes' again for quite a while."

"Who?" asked Isaac, puzzled.

"Angry Eyes," replied Anna, "the baker we met this morning."

"Oh him! I didn't notice his eyes."

"They were horrible, I've never seen eyes looking so angry before!"

"Well, we won't be visiting 'Angry Eyes' for a bit."

As they arrived at the bazaar, Anna felt nervous. "Don't worry, just stick with me," Isaac reassured her.

Isaac, it turned out, was good at begging. He seemed to know just who to ask for money. Many people ignored him, and some shouted, he even got a cuff around the ear, but a few did give him money.

"Wow! That's more than I normally get," he said, "I think it helped having you with me."

For the first time since arriving in Jerusalem, Anna's stomach felt full. With the extra money, they had been able to buy more bread than usual. Anna also felt safer, Isaac seemed so confident, and his confidence was beginning to rub off on her.

That night they hid and slept in a newer stable, which was quite a luxury as it had a lot of fresh, clean straw in it.

"You have to choose somewhere different each night so it's less noticeable," Isaac had explained, "then there's less chance of slave traders finding you."

The next morning, they woke up feeling refreshed having slept a little better.

"I'm really thirsty," said Anna, "we'd better go to the well and get a drink."

"Ok, we'll use your goatskin, it's good that you have one," said Isaac.

"How have you managed without one?" asked Anna.

Isaac shrugged "Oh, you know, I borrow things, most people will lend me something to drink out of, if not, I use my hands."

Anna admired Isaac's nonchalant attitude. He did not seem to worry about anything. She felt permanently on the brink of panic herself. She was already worrying about where they would sleep that night, and how cold it would be, even with Isaac's cloak.

"I wish I still had my blanket," she sighed.

"What happened to your blanket?" Isaac asked.

"I lost it on my first day here, I left it in an alleyway when I ran away from a man who was shouting at me, I was scared he might be a slave trader."

"Do the slave traders who are after you even know what you look like?" asked Isaac.

"I think so, I mean I recognised them, so they would probably recognise me as we've met before. I thought they were friends of my dad, but it turns out they just lent him some money!"

"So, what do they look like?"

"Well, one of them only has one hand now, and he's tall and dark and his eyes are close together and I've never seen him smile. The other one is a bit smaller but much wider and he has a horrible scar going down his face which makes him look really scary! I was always scared when I saw them," Anna shivered involuntarily as she described the men.

"Well, we'll keep an eye out for them, don't worry I'll keep you safe," said Isaac sounding braver than he felt, "let's go and get some water."

They strolled to the well, there was no rush when your only plan for the day was to eat enough to stay alive!

"So, Anna, what do you fancy for breakfast?" asked Isaac grandly, after they had had their fill of water.

Anna smiled, "Well actually, I'd love a nice piece of fish and some freshly baked bread followed by some figs," she joked, "what about you?"

"Sounds good!" said Isaac, playing along. That was not the sort of breakfast either of them had ever had! He led the way back to the bazaar and they began begging again.

It was crowded and noisy, as always. Anna hated begging. Most people ignored their pleas for money or food, some people shouted at them, one man even pushed Anna roughly out of his way! After this, Anna hid behind Isaac most of the time. They did not get any breakfast; and by the time they had enough money to buy some bread, it was lunchtime, and their stomachs were rumbling. However, an unexpected bonus came their way when one of the table legs of a fruit stall collapsed and sent all kinds of fruit rolling on the ground.

Isaac and Anna were very quick to gather up the stray fruit and give it back to the grateful stallholder who rewarded them each with a handful of soft ripe figs and grapes.

"That was delicious!" said Anna as she wiped the grape juice from her chin and licked her grubby hand, not wishing to waste any.

Hunger satisfied, the children wandered up onto the hillside and sat down overlooking the temple.

"Did you ever go to temple?" asked Anna.

"Sometimes, with my mum, for special occasions. I also went to the synagogue occasionally, to be taught by the rabbi; but I didn't like it much, and my mum needed help at home, so I stayed with her most of the time."

"Have you ever met Jesus?" asked Anna.

"Who?"

"Jesus. Have you heard of him?"

"Do you mean that man who's supposedly going around healing the sick and annoying the elders and chief priest's cos he's telling lies about God?"

"Yes, except he's not telling lies and he is healing sick people, I saw him."

Isaac spun round to look at her, "You mean it's true? I thought it was a rumour. What's he like?"

"Well, you know 'Angry Eyes' the baker?" Isaac nodded with a grin.

"He's the complete opposite! I was with my dad, and we listened to him for a while. He spoke about God, he called him his father, he talked about him as if he knew him really well; you know, as if he'd actually seen him and lived with him. And he said God was our Father and he loved us very much. And he played some games with us children, and he smiled at us, and he healed a man who was blind, so he could actually see; it was amazing! And then there was a woman who had something wrong with her leg and he put his hand on her shoulder and she started walking and jumping saying she was cured, and everyone was amazed! Then there was another man who had a small, withered hand and Jesus made it grow into a normal hand and I actually saw it grow, and then some religious leaders started arguing with him because he was healing people on the sabbath, and they said he shouldn't do that," Anna was so animated; her words were rapidly tumbling out with almost no pause for breath, "so that's when my dad dragged me away; he said that the religious leaders were being hypocrites, but he wasn't sure if Jesus was telling the truth either but I think he was - telling the truth that is. If you'd seen his eyes! The way he looked at me. It was like I was the only person in the world, like he knew me, like he really loved me. Sometimes I wonder if he's looking after me right now. I just wish I could meet him again. Maybe he could help us!" Anna suddenly became silent, thinking about Jesus, she completely forgot Isaac was there.

"Hello? Are you still with me?" asked Isaac.

"What? Oh sorry, I was just remembering that's all."

Anna began to have an idea about searching for Jesus, she could not get him out of her mind; the way he spoke and laughed, his eyes – she had never seen anything like them. The compassion he had when he healed the blind man, the tenderness with which he spoke to the children. Suddenly, she longed to find him, she felt that if she could just see him again, he could make everything all right. She said as much to Isaac.

"Well, it's not like we're really busy and can't spare the time," he replied, "but I just don't know how we would even start to search for him. I mean you said he moves around going from place to place. How did you find him the first time?"

"I'm not sure, I just went with my dad, he'd heard a few things and he spoke to a few people, then we saw crowds of people and there he was."

They mulled things over for a while, neither of them having any idea how to find Jesus.

"We could go to the temple and see if we could find out something about Jesus," suggested Isaac.

"Did you go right inside the temple when you went with your mum?" Anna asked.

"No, not right inside, just around the outside."

"What's it like?"

"It's huge and it's not even finished yet! King Herod started to build it years ago. I've only been in the outer court, I heard someone say it was called the 'Court of the Gentiles'. It's the place where people who aren't Jewish can go and it has stalls in it where people sell things, particularly animals used for sacrifices. Sometimes people stand up and start talking about God and our Jewish history and others sit down and listen to them. But there are parts that you should see! Some of it is made of this beautiful smooth cream coloured marble and some bits are gold!"

"Wow!" said Anna "I'd like to see that. Can we go inside the actual temple?"

"I'm not sure, I don't think so, there's parts only the priests can go in, and I know there's a place for women. But we can go and have a look."

"I'd like that, but I'm not sure if we'll find out anything about Jesus because my dad said that the priests don't like him, and they won't have anything to do with him. He heard them say that Jesus was not telling the truth and people shouldn't listen to anything he said ."

"Do you really think he was telling the truth then?" asked Isaac sceptically.

"I do! Oh, if only you could see Jesus, Isaac! Even my dad said he'd never heard anyone like him. In some ways he was like no-one I've ever met; in other ways he was so normal. The way he said things...even I could understand what he was saying! And no-one could deny the miracles he did. I really want to see him again."

"Well, now we've had lunch, let's get going to the temple and see what we can find out."

They walked down the hillside and wove their way through a few alleyways and side streets. The temple was further away than it seemed, but Isaac really knew his way around and Anna told him so.

"I've been around a lot," he replied, puffing out his chest.

"Have you ever come across other children like us?" asked Anna.

"Oh yeah, there's a few about, you have seen them, but they've learnt to blend into the crowd. I've seen some of them attach themselves to families, so it looks like they're with them."

"Have you ever seen a slave trader take a child?" worried Anna.

"Only once," Isaac's face fell.

Anna gasped, "What happened?"

"It was only a couple of weeks after I was kicked out of home. I was hiding behind some old baskets having just run away from a man who got angry with me for asking for money, and I saw this small girl get taken. At first, they were quite nice to her and said they could offer her a better life - you know, food to eat and somewhere to live. When she refused, they grabbed hold of her. She screamed, but they just took her. I never saw her again, I wish I could have done something, I don't think it would have been a better life." Isaac went quiet, and Anna saw a glint of a tear in the corner of his eye, it was clearly a painful memory.

Anna shivered involuntarily again. Isaac noticed it was the second time she had done that when they talked about slave traders. Anna glanced around as though looking for any signs of danger.

"Sometimes the Romans just make people their slaves, some people even willingly sell themselves as slaves," remarked Isaac.

"I know, I've heard of that! Sometimes, people think being a slave is better than begging on the streets. I mean, how desperate do you have to be to believe that?"

"Well, I suppose if you've got no money or food, you don't have a lot of choice. I mean, some people rely on begging to get food for their whole lives - you know, if they're crippled or something and can't get work. I suppose those people wouldn't even have the option of being slaves. But at least if you're a slave you get food, clothing and somewhere to live."

"We won't have to do that, will we Isaac?"

"Not if I can help it! We'll beg while we must and as soon as I can, I'll find some work. We'll get by somehow."

"I really hope we can stay away from the slave traders!" Anna shuddered, looking around for fear that someone might be listening.

"Me too," said Isaac, "anyway, we're almost there."

"How do we get in?" Anna asked looking at the wall surrounding the temple.

"This way, there's some steps leading to a couple of gates."

Isaac and Anna went in unnoticed amongst the throngs of visitors, people going in and out of the temple courts. They wandered around the edge of the temple on a paved pathway that they had overheard someone call "Solomon's Porch". Isaac pointed to the hillside through some archways, "That's the Mount of Olives over there."

"I don't think we can get very near to the temple, it's got another wall around it," said Anna, disappointed.

"Let's find the Court of the Gentiles, we should be able to go in there," replied Isaac.

They retraced their steps and came to the walled area of the Court of the Gentiles. Anna was surprised; it was nothing like she expected! It was bustling with life! It was basically a marketplace with money lenders and people shouting, selling their wares, mainly animals that people could use for sacrifice. Anna had expected it to be quieter with people showing more respect.

Both children looked up when they heard some raised voices. Two men were arguing:

"But that's an extortionate rate of interest! I would be paying you back twice what I borrowed!" one man said.

"Up to you sir, you need the money, I have the money, that's what it will cost you to borrow from me!" said the second, a rather well-dressed man.

Anna did not like the look of the man lending the money. She remembered her father telling her how wicked some of the money lenders were and how they forced you to pay back so much more money than you had borrowed in the first place. He had said it was downright evil. So why had he borrowed money? His money lenders were even more ruthless than this one appeared to be. Anna shuddered at the thought, "Let's get away from here," she said to Isaac.

They looked around the parts of the temple that they could get to, and Anna enjoyed running her hands over the smooth marble, she was fascinated by it. After about half an hour, the two children decided they had had enough as they were getting hungry, and they had not had the courage to ask anyone about Jesus as everyone was either in a hurry or seemed unfriendly.

"Now, I know you don't like stealing, but I know of a bread stall a little way from here that is the easiest place in the world to steal from, the stallholder doesn't notice anything."

"Isaac no! It's not worth the risk! Please don't!"

"Anna, trust me, remember when we were at 'Angry Eyes' place and I told you there was one other place safe to steal from? Well, this is it. I promise you, it's safe. You can stand at a distance and watch if it makes you feel any better."

Anna reluctantly followed Isaac as they walked out of the temple back down the steps, once again weaving in and out of alleyways until they eventually got to the bazaar; Anna decided Isaac had a different definition of "a little way"- it had seemed to take ages!

"Right, you stay here and watch this," said Isaac.

"I can't watch," said Anna, turning away.

"Suit yourself," said Isaac as he walked towards a bread stall.

But despite her misgivings, Anna could not help herself and she watched Isaac brazenly walk up to the bread stall and take some bread. He did not even try to hide what he was doing. She held her breath as she saw the stallholder look directly at Isaac and watch him steal the bread! Her heart was thumping as she expected him to grab hold of Isaac or at least chase after him, but instead, the man smiled to himself and served the next customer.

This man knew full well that some children were stealing from him, but he felt sorry for the poor little mites, and if he could help by occasionally pretending not to notice, then he would!

"He saw you!" Anna hissed at Isaac as he approached her.

"No, he didn't, he doesn't see anything!"

"Isaac, I saw what happened, he was watching you and he just smiled and let you have the bread!"

Isaac was not convinced, but Anna was sure of what she had seen. She let the matter drop however, as she was too hungry to argue, "I wish I knew which direction my home was in," she mumbled as she was eating.

"Which gate did you come through to get into the city?" asked Isaac through a mouthful of bread.

"I've no idea, I was hidden in the back of a cart with a sack covering me, and even if I wasn't, I don't think I would know as it all looks the same to me!"

The two children ate silently, and Anna began to think about her journey to Jerusalem and how she had had to say goodbye to Mary. She wondered if Mary was worrying about her. She decided she probably was.

Anna was right, Mary was worrying.

"I wish I knew if she was safe," Mary said to herself as she stood in her little home wringing her hands. She had spoken to Zechariah upon his return from Jerusalem.

"Mary, I don't know what to tell you, I don't know what happened to Anna after she ran off, and no, I don't think anyone saw her in the cart." Zechariah had decided not to mention the time when Anna had thrown off the sack and tried to persuade him to take her to see Jesus, he did not want to give Mary anything else to worry about.

Mary, however, was right to worry.

The one-handed man and his scar-faced companion who were looking for Anna, had gone back to Jerusalem where they lived. By chance, as they arrived at the gates of Jerusalem, Zechariah and his friends were just leaving to return home. The two men recognised Zechariah from their trips to the village and decided to question him to see if he knew anything about Anna. However, as they approached him, one of Zechariah's companions called out to Zechariah, "where's that young girl who came up with you to Jerusalem?"

Zechariah looked flustered as he answered, "Oh, she's staying on in Jerusalem." he said evasively and quickly increased his pace to avoid further conversation.

An evil grin spread across the one-handed man's face, "So, she's in Jerusalem!" he muttered to his companion, turning away before Zechariah noticed them.

"We'll never find her in Jerusalem," the other one said, "there are thousands of people here!"

But the first man was obsessed with getting his money back and would not let it rest, he blamed Anna's father, John, for losing his hand. If John had paid the money back sooner, he would have been able to pay his debt in full to the other slavers and would not have had his hand taken in part payment. According to him, John had ruined his life, and seeing as John was dead and he could not get any more from him, he was determined to get his revenge on John by capturing and selling Anna as a slave. He intended to keep looking for her, after all, he knew what she looked like as they had seen Anna with John on a number of occasions.

"Ok, I'll help you look but I'm not spending a lot of time on it," the scar-faced man had reluctantly agreed, "we've got plenty of other business that needs our attention." he grinned wickedly.

Chapter Five

The Triumphal Entry

In Jerusalem, the days turned into weeks for Isaac and Anna. They managed to survive by begging for food or money and occasionally by picking wild figs from the trees on the hills. It was a hard way of life for the two young children and some days they did not eat at all, as they had long since spent the remainder of Anna's money. Every night they found a different place to sleep, sometimes it was an old, abandoned building, sometimes just a hard floor somewhere near a wall, or sometimes amongst some old baskets that had been left discarded and forgotten in a quiet alleyway.

They had heard rumours of Jesus. Stories of his teaching and healing. But they had no idea where to find him. It seemed from the stories that Jesus was moving about from place to place, and no-one knew where he would be next. It was far too dangerous for Isaac and Anna to leave the city to look for Jesus, especially when they had no idea where he was.

Anna's hopes of meeting Jesus began to fade as the days dragged on. Then suddenly, one day they heard an excited babble of voices.

"Jesus is on his way to Jerusalem!"

"Everyone's coming out to see him!"

"He's riding on a donkey!"

All through the city people were talking about Jesus and beginning to move towards one of the gates in anticipation. Some of them declared him to be the saviour that God had promised to rescue the Jews from their enemies. At the moment, their enemies were the Romans who had invaded and ruled their cities and demanded that they pay taxes.

"He's going to overthrow the Roman government!"

"God has always promised us a saviour!"

"He's going to free us from the Romans!"

"No more paying taxes to Caesar!"

"I wonder if he'll heal some people?"

Isaac and Anna looked at each other.

"We'll get to see him!" squealed Anna, her face alight with excitement.

"I hope so!" replied Isaac, for by now he was desperate to see this man that Anna had talked about so much. He was not sure what he believed about Jesus, but Anna seemed convinced that he was someone special. Isaac was determined to make up his own mind.

They followed the crowds out of the city gates, comfortable with leaving the relative safety and anonymity of the city during the day, because they were among so many other people.

Anna could barely contain her excitement. She was clinging on to Isaac's hand as they were afraid of losing each other in the growing press of people. They walked with the crowd until they heard someone shout above the noise.

"There he is! Look!"

They squeezed their way through to the edge of the roadway and waited eagerly. Anna did not even realise that she was hopping up and down in excitement, almost pulling Isaac off his feet. Isaac laughed and let go of her hand.

As Jesus approached, sitting astride a donkey, people in the crowd began to shout, "Hosanna to the son of David!"

Some people were laying palm branches down on the ground in front of the donkey and others, who had no palm branches were laying their cloaks on the dusty ground for the donkey to walk on. Jesus' disciples were with him, Anna recognised some of them, they looked a little astounded at the crowd's reaction.

Isaac and Anna watched as Jesus drew nearer. Anna had butterflies in her stomach; would he see her? Would he remember her amongst the crowd? She wanted to call out to Jesus but found that she could not speak, such was her excitement and nervousness. What if Jesus had changed? She had placed a lot of hope in him; what if she had misremembered?

But Anna need not have worried. As the donkey passed, Jesus turned his head in her direction and met her gaze. He smiled and for a fleeting moment Anna felt as though she was the only person in the world with Jesus. In that instant she felt known and loved.

"Did you see that?" Anna tugged at Isaac's sleeve.

"Yeah, he looked at us, so what?" said Isaac dismissively. Just one look did not prove to him that Jesus was anything special. He had got caught up with the crowd's excitement, seen their adoration of Jesus, but he was not convinced himself. However, he did not want to disappoint Anna, so he let her babble on excitedly about Jesus as they followed the crowd back through the gates into Jerusalem.

"I wonder where he's going?" questioned Isaac.

"I don't know, but let's try and see."

They followed the crowd as much as they could, but it was impossible to stay near to Jesus through the narrow streets. They seemed to be drawing close to the temple. There was a growing mix of emotions in the crowd, some were full of anticipation, but some even seemed disappointed.

"I thought he'd come to overthrow the government, what's he doing at the temple?" they heard someone say.

Anna thought about this, it would be great to be free of the Romans. The soldiers that were everywhere, made Anna nervous. She had witnessed many people shrink back out of the soldiers' way when they marched past. But there were so many of them in Jerusalem, how could Jesus and his men possibly fight them? The whole idea filled her with fear.

Isaac and Anna fought their way through the crowds to get into the temple courts. As they entered the courts they heard a commotion, and what they saw astounded them! Instead of sitting down and teaching the people, Jesus was on his feet amongst the traders and money lenders. There were tables on their sides, money scattered on the floor and animals escaping from their cages. They heard a crash as Jesus turned over the table of the money lender they had seen before, and then Jesus chased him out of the temple courts with a whip!

"How dare you treat my Father's house like a market-place!" he cried.

Anna saw the fire in his eyes and the people who were watching seemed stunned at what he was doing.

"I've never seen him this angry before," a woman said.

Isaac and Anna were totally shocked at what they were seeing.

"I'm really beginning to like your Jesus!" Isaac said to Anna, grinning as he watched one of the money lenders running away.

As the disturbance seemed to be increasing, and the temple guards started to push through the crowd, Isaac took hold of Anna's hand, "Come on," said he said as he pulled her away, "we need to find some food and somewhere to sleep tonight."

Anna reluctantly allowed herself to be led away.

Later that night, after filling up on stale bread given to them by a stallholder, the two children sat on the hillside overlooking the city and spoke about the day.

"I wonder if Jesus will stay in Jerusalem for a while?" mused Anna, "I want to see him again, I really think he can help us!"

"I overheard someone say he was going to be around for the Passover feast at the end of the week," replied Isaac.

"What's the Passover feast? Why is it called Passover?" asked Anna.

"Oh, I know this one!" said Isaac excitedly, "We learnt about it in the synagogue. You've heard about Moses, right?"

"Yes, I know God used Moses to rescue the Israelites out of Egypt."

"Okay, do you remember about the plagues that God inflicted on Pharaoh and the Egyptians because he wouldn't let the Israelites go?"

Anna looked uncertain.

"Well, the first nine plagues that God sent were things like frogs, flies, gnats, locusts, darkness, illness, etc; well, when Pharaoh still refused to let them go, God sent a final plague, it was a plague of death on all the first-born boys and animals of the Egyptians. Moses told the Israelites to sacrifice a lamb, paint their doorways with its blood, cook it and eat it and then go inside their house and shut the door. Then at midnight the angel of death would go through Egypt and when he saw the blood of the lambs on the doors of the Israelites he would pass over those houses and so the plague would only affect the Egyptians. That's why it's called the Passover because the angel passed over their houses."

"Ah, I see, I get it now! I remember celebrating that with my dad and Mary and her family once," said Anna, "Now I know why we had lamb, I think that's the only time I've eaten lamb, I really enjoyed it! Mary's son brought it and she cooked it; it was delicious! I can't remember the last time I had any meat."

"Me neither," said Isaac, "it was always a luxury even when I did have a home to live in! So, where will we celebrate Passover this year? And how would you like your lamb cooked?"

Anna giggled, "I wish we could have a Passover meal and eat lamb."

"I wonder if we could get some lamb?"

"Not likely!" laughed Anna, "and I don't know how to cook it anyway, and where would we cook it?"

"Okay, I was only kidding!"

They decided to move further up the hillside to their favourite place, a disused stable. "I prefer to be up here out of the way," said Isaac as they settled down for the night. "Me too," said Anna as she wriggled around trying to get comfortable on some straw.

"Maybe we should stay here every night. It is the most comfortable place we sleep in," suggested Isaac.

"But what if people see us? You said we should keep moving around!"

"Yeah, I know, it's just that I get tired of sleeping rough and this is the closest thing to a house, it even has part of a roof!"

"I know, I like it too, but do you think it would be okay to stay here every night?"

"I don't know, let's talk about it in the morning," yawned Isaac, "I'm really tired."

The children lay down on the small amount of straw on the dusty floor and Anna pulled the cloak over herself. Although it was hot during the day, it did get quite cold at night, so the children were grateful for the shelter. Isaac seemed to fall asleep straight away, his gentle snoring a strange comfort to Anna, but despite this, she had trouble sleeping that night; she was tired, but she could not stop thinking about Jesus, "I wonder if he will rescue us from the Romans like God rescued the Israelites out of Egypt?" she thought to herself.

When Anna awoke the next morning and stretched, she looked around for Isaac but could not see him; she was completely alone! Panicking, she raced to the doorway and looked around for him, both up and down the hill, but he was nowhere to be seen.

She was too scared to call out in case someone had taken him and was still nearby. Anna shrank back into the shadows and hugged her knees, once again rocking backwards and forwards in distress.

"What's the matter?" asked Isaac appearing at the doorway.

"Where were you?" sobbed Anna, "I looked for you, I thought you'd been taken!"

"Hey, calm down, I'm sorry, shhh, it's okay!" Isaac comforted Anna,

"I tried to wake you, you even opened your eyes and looked at me and I told you I was going to fetch some water."

"You did?"

"Yes, I thought you'd heard me!"

"I don't remember that!" cried Anna.

It took quite a while for Anna to calm down after such a fright.

"Look, Anna," said Isaac, "I promise that I will never abandon you. But it's going to get even more crowded in Jerusalem as the Passover feast approaches, and there will be thousands of extra people in the city, so we may end up getting separated. We need to have a plan."

"What do you mean?" asked Anna.

"Well, if we find ourselves separated and we can't find one another, we both head for this place and wait here until the other one turns up, right?"

"Okay."

"And I've been thinking, it's probably not a good idea to stay here every night after all; it would be best to keep moving around." Isaac was not going to tell Anna, but when he had gone to fetch the water, he had seen two men matching the description of her slave traders. He decided to take a risk and get closer to see if he could overhear their conversation. He got as close as he could without being seen, and listened:

"I don't know why you don't just give up; you're never going to find her amongst all these people," said the shorter, two-handed man with a scar down his face.

"I've told you; I want revenge!" the other man held up his arm with the missing hand.

"But he's dead now, and if we don't pay off the rest of your debt, you'll lose the other hand, or worse!" 'Scar-face' was becoming angry.

"You do what you want, I'm going to find this girl and use her to clear my debt if it's the last thing I do! We know she was brought to Jerusalem, it's just a matter of time, she'll turn up."

"Are you kidding? There are thousands of people here! We'll never find her!" replied 'Scar- face', exasperated.

The one-handed man just glared and walked away.

"Alright!" 'Scar-face' conceded, "We'll keep looking." he said as he sullenly followed his companion.

Isaac had been horrified when he heard this exchange. What he had just overheard was too similar to Anna's story, to be a coincidence. He decided there and then not to tell her as she was already frightened enough.

"So, what do you feel like doing today?" Isaac asked Anna.

"I would really love it if we could find Jesus again," Anna replied.

"Okay, but he could be anywhere, he may not even still be in Jerusalem."

"I know, but what else have we got to do except beg for food?"

"Okay then, we can look for Jesus while we're trying to get money or food," said Isaac.

By the end of the day, Anna's feet were sore. They had walked for miles unsuccessfully looking for Jesus, and Isaac had been unusually nervous, constantly looking around.

"What's up with you today?" Anna had asked.

"Nothing, why?"

"You seem a bit worried, you're not as relaxed as normal."

"I'm fine," Isaac said brusquely, and that was all she could get out of him. The following day was much the same, as was the next.

But on the fourth day of looking, they found Jesus. It was hard to get close, but they squeezed through the crowds somehow, and watched as Jesus spoke to a man sitting on the ground.

The man was clearly a cripple, his legs looked thin and withered and were folded underneath him. They could not hear what Jesus was saying but they saw the man's face begin to brighten as he listened to Jesus. The man nodded his head and Jesus reached out and took him by the hand. The crowd gasped as they watched the man stand up, his legs suddenly strong and whole. The man gingerly took a step, and then another, and another! Soon, he began to leap about, all over the place, totally undignified, praising God for his healing. The crowd clapped and cheered; Jesus laughed at the man's delight.

"Whoa! Did you see that?" Isaac turned to Anna, excitement in his eyes, "He just put his hand out to that man and made him walk! And I know it's true because I've seen that man before being carried by his friends to that spot, so that he can beg for money. Look at him leaping around!"

Anna turned to Isaac, beaming, "I told you Jesus was special, there isn't anything he can't do!"

The children then found themselves being pushed roughly aside by a couple of men who were trying to get closer to Jesus. But they did not look happy, in fact they looked even angrier than 'Angry Eyes' the baker.

"One of those men is a Chief Priest, I've seen him around the temple," Isaac whispered to Anna, "you told me the priests don't like Jesus."

"I don't know why they seem so angry; you'd think they'd be pleased that someone was talking about God and healing people. Although I do remember my dad telling me that a lot of people didn't believe anything that Jesus said. I heard Jesus call some of those religious leaders, hypocrites!" replied Anna.

"Well, I think some of them are! I've seen some of them wandering around thinking they're better than everyone else. Besides, how can Jesus be wrong if he's doing miracles?"

"I don't know, but..." Anna was interrupted by the same two men pushing back through the crowd; she and Isaac caught part of their conversation: "...yes, but it will have to be at night when he's alone or only with his disciples, the crowd wouldn't let us take him in broad daylight. This has got to stop, it's blasphemy!"

Isaac and Anna looked at one another horrified, "They were talking about Jesus, weren't they?" whispered Anna, "We have to warn him! What does he mean by blasphemy?"

Isaac did not reply but grabbed Anna by the hand and forced his way through the crowd to try to get to Jesus, but the crowd was too thick and by the time they had battled their way through, Jesus had moved on and was nowhere in sight.

"What shall we do?" worried Anna, "We have to tell him!"

"I don't think there's anything we can do!" replied Isaac, "Come on, let's get out of here."

The two children left the crowd and wandered aimlessly, not really knowing what to do. They both wished they could tell someone about what they had heard, maybe an adult who would know how to get a message to Jesus.

"What about the man who lets you steal his bread? You know, the one who pretends not to see you, he must be a nice man, we could talk to him."

"I don't know," replied Isaac, "what if he's really horrible like 'Angry Eyes'?"

"He's not, I know he's not, we should at least try," pleaded Anna.

"Anna let's just leave it please! Remember, you told me once that Jesus said he is God's son, so I'm sure he can take care of himself, and if he can't, then surely God will look after his own son."

Anna thought that Isaac made a good point, but it did not stop her fretting and once again she had trouble sleeping that night, as they hid amongst some old baskets propped against the wall of a building.

The next morning when the children woke early as soon as the sun had risen, they were at a complete loss as to what to do. Anna was keen to try and find Jesus again, but Isaac was more concerned about keeping Anna out of the public eye in case she was seen by the slave traders.

He was still not going to tell her this, though, as he felt she had enough on her mind. Different worries meant that neither of them were particularly hungry that morning, but knowing they needed to eat, Isaac managed to scrounge a couple of bruised apples from a reluctant stallholder which they forced themselves to eat.

By the end of that week, Anna was frantic, "We have to find Jesus! What if they've already taken him?"

Isaac decided he could not take any more of Anna's nagging, "Okay, okay, I don't know where Jesus is, but we can go and see our friend who lets me steal bread." Isaac had finally conceded that the man at the stall was not clueless but had been turning a blind eye to his stealing.

They set off and soon found their way to the stallholder. They had to wait for the early morning customers to buy their bread before they could talk to their 'friend' alone.

The stallholder looked at the children, he had seen them many times and had actually felt sorry for them. He assumed that they were either orphans or came from extremely poor families as they both looked so neglected and malnourished.

"Hello, you two," the stallholder had a soft, gentle voice, "How can I help you today? Don't tell me you actually want to buy something?"

Anna noticed the twinkle in his eye and the corner of his lip turning up into a smile. Suddenly, she felt a bit braver about talking to him, "Do you know Jesus, have you seen him?" Anna blurted out before Isaac had a chance to answer.

The stallholder was a little taken aback but quickly recovered and replied, "Well, actually I have seen him, I've even been healed by him. I was deaf in my left ear, and Jesus put his hand on it and suddenly I could hear again! But I don't know where he is now, Jesus doesn't tend to stay in one place for long. Why are you looking for him?"

"We heard something," said Isaac, "and we need to warn Jesus." Isaac was a little wary of telling the stallholder too much just in case he was a friend of the chief priests.

Anna, however, was convinced he was not, "The chief priests are out to get him! They said something about blasphemy!" she exclaimed.

The stallholder beckoned them closer, "Why don't you tell me all about it?"

Isaac and Anna felt they had no choice but to trust him and they moved closer so that they could talk quietly. They relayed what they had heard at the temple and were a little shocked when the man - who told them his name was Stephen - did not react in the way they thought he would. He laughed! The children were horrified and stood there with their mouths open, unable to speak. Did Stephen think they were making it up?

"I'm sorry," said Stephen, "I believe what you say is true, but I've met Jesus. You don't need to worry about him. He knows the chief priests want to kill him; they've been trying to find ways to get him for ages. They've accused him of blasphemy because he said he's God's son – I happen to believe he is and I'm sure he could call down a whole host of angels to protect himself if he wanted to! Now, have some bread, run along, and don't worry. I've got customers to serve."

And with that, Stephen loaded them up with some lovely fresh bread and turned to serve his customers.

Not knowing what else to do, Isaac and Anna took the bread and slipped away.

"Do you know, I think his bread tastes better when it's not stolen!" laughed Isaac later as they sat down to eat under the shade of a fig tree just outside of the city where many people were milling about, going in and out of the gate.

"It really does!" said Anna wiping her mouth. "So, do you think Stephen was right? Will Jesus be okay?"

"I hope so," replied Isaac, "if he is the son of God, then surely he's got God on his side." Anna remained uncertain and still wished she could find some way to warn Jesus.

Isaac suddenly stiffened as he saw two men coming out of the city gates. He recognised them as the slave traders who were looking for Anna. Isaac stood up quickly and pulled Anna behind some nearby rocks.

"What are you doing Isaac? What's wrong?" asked Anna, alarmed.

"There were some people looking at us, I don't like being noticed."

Anna was confused, it seemed like an overreaction on Isaac's part, but she stayed behind the rocks until Isaac said it was okay to come out, "They've moved on now, it was probably nothing," he said trying to sound casual, "let's go back into the city."

"I was enjoying sitting under the fig tree," said Anna, grumpily. But Isaac just ignored her and led her back down the hill and through the city gates.

They spent the rest of the afternoon wandering around the bazaar telling one another what they would buy if they had enough money. Their imaginations went wild, and their shopping lists became more and more ridiculous as time went on!

As evening drew in, Isaac did not want to go outside of the city gates where he had seen the slave traders, so they found a quiet alleyway and settled down to sleep. Although the ground was hard, within a few moments both children had fallen fast asleep.

Chapter six

The End of Hope

It was still dark when Anna was awoken by a commotion nearby, "Wake up, Isaac!" she shook him awake.

"W ...what is it?" yawned Isaac.

"Can't you hear? Good grief, Isaac, I think you would sleep through an earthquake!"

"What's happening?" Isaac asked again, wide awake by now.

"I don't know, lots of people shouting. Something's going on!"

Isaac crawled out of his makeshift bed and looked out, "Let's go see!"

They followed the sound of the noise, weaving their way through the alleyways in the moonlight and came upon a gathering crowd of people. They tried in vain to see what was causing the commotion, but it was too dark and there were too many people in front of them.

Isaac tried to speak to Anna, but it was very noisy, so instead he grabbed her hand and led her back to some steps which they climbed to give them a higher vantage point. What they saw horrified them.

Standing with the chief priests and Pilate the Roman Governor, his hands bound, his head bruised and bloodied with a crown made of thorns - was Jesus.

Neither child could speak. Dumbstruck, they stood and watched as Jesus was accused of blasphemy and other charges which they could not hear above the noise of the crowd. But they did hear Pilate offering the people a choice, he could either release Jesus or another prisoner - Barabbas, a murderer. They could scarcely believe their ears as the crowd yelled for the release of Barabbas.

"Do something, Jesus!" shouted Anna, "We should have warned him!" Anna was distraught and desperate. She felt so helpless, there was nothing she could do! Then the crowd started to shout, "Crucify him!"

Jesus was led away by some soldiers, and the mob followed. Isaac and Anna stayed where they were.

"I don't understand..." sobbed Anna.

"Nor do I," replied Isaac putting his arm around her shoulder.

"Why are they being so horrible? Why doesn't Jesus stop them? They won't really crucify him, will they?" Anna had unfortunately seen people crucified, it was unavoidable in Jerusalem or anywhere the Romans occupied. It was the cruellest of executions; those convicted of sometimes a small crime would be nailed to a wooden cross and left to eventually die by suffocation. It could take hours and hours for someone to die, and the Romans seemed to enjoy lining the roads with the victims of their "justice" for all to see as a deterrent to stop others committing crimes. Anna hated it!

Dawn light began to fill the sky. Isaac did not know what to say to Anna. He knew that they would crucify Jesus unless a miracle happened and he desperately tried to think of a way to protect Anna from that brutal reality, but he knew she would find out eventually even if he could shield her from it right now.

"Isaac! What should we do?" Anna tugged at his sleeve.

"We should get away from here."

"No, we have to follow them, find out where they're taking him. Come on, Isaac."

Isaac grabbed her hand, "No Anna, I'm sorry this is all getting too dangerous, we need to get out of here."

Anna reluctantly allowed Isaac to lead her away. The city gates had just been opened, so Isaac took Anna through the gates and up onto the hillside. They sat down overlooking the city. Isaac tried to distract her, but she just sat staring straight ahead, biting her lip anxiously. Isaac became quite worried when he could get no response from her as he tried to get her to talk.

"Come on Anna, it'll be okay. Anna, you're starting to worry me now, say something please!"

Eventually Anna looked at Isaac and spoke. She was strangely calm, "We need to go back and find out what's happening to Jesus."

"I don't think that's a good idea"

"Yes, it is. You'll see. Jesus will call some angels to rescue him and then he will carry on teaching people and healing the sick and everything will go back to normal," she said defiantly.

"Anna..."

"You just don't believe in him like I do Isaac; trust me, you'll see..."

"Anna, stop! I wish that what you're saying would happen, but even Jesus can't escape now. He was surrounded by soldiers as well as a mob of people who were really angry with him and wanted to kill him!"

Anna began to feel really cross with Isaac; he just did not understand! She sprang up and began to run back down the hill towards the city gates.

"Anna, wait!" Isaac ran after her and very quickly caught her; he grabbed at her arm, but she shook him off and slipped away.

"Anna stop!" He grabbed her arm again and this time he held on tight.

"You have to stop!" he yelled, "Just wait and listen to me! You don't want to see what they're about to do!"

"They won't do it Isaac, they can't.... please tell me they won't. Isaac ... please!" Anna's eyes were pleading as she looked up at Isaac.

More than anything Isaac wanted to lie to her and tell her it would be okay, but he could not, "Anna, I can't say they won't crucify Jesus!"

"Then I want to see him!"

"Okay, I'll take you to the place where they execute criminals, but we won't get too close, and you have to hold my hand, agreed?"

Anna nodded. Isaac led her back down the hill and a short way around the outskirts of the city to another hill. Eventually they came to a halt. Isaac looked up into the distance and saw three large wooden crosses being raised up onto their ends. On each one hung a man, and on the middle cross was Jesus.

Isaac looked at Anna, she had seen the crosses too. "I think this is close enough, we'll stay here, Anna."

She nodded in agreement. They both turned away from the crosses, just occasionally glancing up to see what was going on. Anna cried silent tears, "I don't understand," she sobbed.

Isaac put his arm around her shoulders for the second time that day. He did not know what to say, he wanted to weep like Anna, he felt so helpless. He remembered when he had seen Jesus heal the cripple; at that moment he had believed in Jesus more than at any other time. He had thought Jesus could do anything! But now Jesus just looked like the other men who were hanging on the crosses either side of him.

The children sat down amongst the other people who had gathered to see the execution. Isaac sensed a mix of emotions amongst the spectators. Some were weeping, some were silent, just staring, and some seemed elated that this man was being crucified; at last, they were rid of him!

They stayed where they were for about three hours. Suddenly the sky darkened, as if the sun had been covered.

A frightened hush came over the crowd. It was the middle of the day! Where had the light gone?

Isaac and Anna clung to one another, terrified.

Nobody moved, they were all afraid in the sudden darkness. Some people began to whisper, "I told you he was the son of God."

"This is God's doing, they should not have crucified him!"

For another three hours Isaac and Anna, along with most of the crowd remained where they were.

Then just as suddenly as it had disappeared, the light returned at about three o'clock in the afternoon. The crowd started to murmur. Those who had been sitting down waiting, stood up and looked towards the crosses. A cry of distress rent the air, followed by people crying, shouting, "He's dead!"

All around them, the children heard people talking, crying, shouting, as they received the news that Jesus had died upon the cross.

Isaac and Anna were speechless, numb with grief. How could this have happened? They watched and waited. People started to drift away.

"We should go," Isaac tugged at Anna's arm, but she just shook her head and continued to stare at Jesus' lifeless form. Isaac stared too, unable to drag his gaze away, he did not know what he was expecting to happen.

Isaac took Anna by the hand, "Come on, time to go."

Anna meekly complied, and they walked back into the city. Isaac's stomach began to rumble. They had not eaten anything all day, but neither of them had the energy or desire to beg for food, so they found a place to sleep amongst some old baskets behind a wall and slept fitfully, their minds going over and over the events of the day.

They were up early the next morning despite their lack of sleep. Both children were subdued and barely spoke a word to one another. It was Isaac who pulled himself together first, "Come on Anna, we have to go and get food." He led her by the hand to the edge of a square and left her standing by a wall while he went to beg for some food. After a few unsuccessful attempts, Isaac was given a small loaf of bread by a kind old man. Neither child had much of an appetite, but they ate the bread anyway.

The next few days passed in a haze. Isaac began to worry about Anna as she had barely spoken since Jesus had died. He tried to engage her in conversation about trivial things, but she just nodded or grunted in reply.

It was the fourth day since Jesus had died, when Isaac and Anna were walking through the bazaar and they overheard a conversation between two men, "Good riddance, if you ask me," one of them said.

"It's no more than he deserved. Son of God indeed! Have you heard these ridiculous rumours that are going around? Did you hear that some people are even saying that he came back to life? What nonsense! I heard that the soldiers guarding his tomb stopped his disciples from stealing his body because they were going to pretend he'd risen from the dead !"

"That's not what I heard, apparently the guards were paid off by the chief priests to lie about what happened."

"So, what did happen?"

"I've no idea! But I've seen the religious authorities looking worried and I think they're on the lookout for his disciples to stop them spreading lies about Jesus coming back to life."

"There's no way he's alive!"

"He can't be, if he was alive, surely he would show himself?"

"Exactly! It's just a rumour spread around by his followers. According to my friend, Jesus told his disciples he would die and then come alive again. I think they tried to steal his body to make it look as though he had come alive."

"So, did they steal his body? Is it still in the tomb?"

"I've no idea! But you can't believe half of the rumours you hear." The children heard no more as the men wandered off.

Anna looked at Isaac with excitement in her eyes, "See, I knew he wouldn't die! He's alive! I know it!"

Isaac gave Anna a strained smile. He was so relieved to see her come out of her half-dead state but at the same time was wary of her getting her hopes up based on an overheard conversation about a rumour, "I hope he is, Anna, but we can't know for sure, can we?"

But Anna was not to be deterred, "I just know he's alive, in here," she patted her chest, "I just know."

Isaac decided to let her have her dream, the excitement might keep her going for a few days, but he was worried about what it would do to her if this newfound hope proved false.

Over the next few days, everywhere they went, they looked for Jesus. The city was buzzing with rumours about sightings of Jesus. Some of them seemed so ridiculous that even Anna struggled to believe them. But they did not see him.

Then one day, they overheard a fisherman talking about a miraculous catch of fish up in Galilee, "It was night, I was out in my boat fishing. I'd seen some of the men that were with Jesus out fishing as well. We fished all night, I caught a few fish, but not as many as I hoped for. But they didn't catch a single fish! Then I saw them talking to a man on the shore and he told them to try putting their net over the other side of the boat, so they did and then they hauled in the biggest catch of fish I've ever seen! The net looked like it was about to burst, so several of us had to get out of our own boats to help them drag the net in. I saw them a little bit later and this man on the beach was cooking them some of the fish for breakfast and chatting to them. Some people said it was Jesus, but I don't know. Whoever it was, I don't really care because I got a load of extra fish out of it!"

"A miraculous catch of fish! It's got to be Jesus!" cried Anna, turning to Isaac.

"It sounds like the sort of thing Jesus could do," replied Isaac, "but if it is, it doesn't sound like he's in the city anymore."

"It doesn't matter," said Anna, "I just know he's alive and out there somewhere."

As the days went on though, Anna's hope that she would see Jesus again began to fade. But both children took comfort in their growing belief that Jesus was alive and still doing the kind of things he had always done.

Time passed - several weeks, in fact - and the children still did not see Jesus. There were rumours, plenty of rumours, one even saying that Jesus had now gone back to heaven and that his disciples had watched him go. The children had no idea which rumours were true, if any, but they continued to search for Jesus in Jerusalem, as there was not much else for them to do but beg for money to buy food to survive and find safe places to sleep.

Chapter seven

The Day Everything Changed

It was on the Day of Pentecost, fifty days after the Passover, that everything changed.

The city was heaving with people. Jews from many other parts of Israel and even other nations had gathered in Jerusalem to celebrate the Feast of Harvest.

"Why are there so many people here?" Anna asked Isaac as they fought their way towards a fruit stall at the bazaar.

"I don't know. You know us Jews, we've always got something to celebrate," replied Isaac a little grumpily, as he did not feel at all like celebrating anything right now, "Oh, maybe it's the Feast of Harvest, I've lost track of the days, but I know that's a few weeks after the Passover. I'm not sure. I do think you should hold onto me though, with this many people, we don't want to get separated, and if we do, we meet at our special place, remember?"

"Yes, I remember."

Isaac had grown more relaxed over the last couple of weeks as he had seen no sign of the slave traders and he had begun to hope that they had given up trying to find Anna. He took Anna's hand and pushed his way to the fruit stall to buy some apples. Begging had been easy today, people were in a good mood and feeling generous, so the children could buy bread and fruit as a treat.

As Isaac and Anna wandered around munching on their apples, a sudden commotion further down the street piqued their curiosity. They came to the edge of a large square and saw hundreds of people, craning their necks to look at something. As Isaac and Anna drew closer, struggling to see what had attracted the crowd's attention, they heard a confused babble of sound. They began to distinguish men and women's voices crying out words in languages that they did not understand. It sounded like there were many different languages being spoken.

Isaac and Anna squeezed through the crowd to see who was responsible for all the commotion.

"I recognise those men," shouted Anna to Isaac. "They're Jesus' disciples!"

Someone close to them started sneering and suggested that the disciples must be drunk on wine. They overheard another man telling his friend in a strange accent that he could understand one of the languages and that the disciples were saying wonderful things about God. Others were saying that these were just ordinary uneducated men, so how could they have learnt these other languages?

Suddenly a hush fell over the crowd as one of the disciples stepped forward and started to speak, "We are not drunk, as some of you think we are," he said, "it is only nine o'clock in the morning!"

This disciple spoke very boldly, not holding anything back when he reminded the Jews that it was they who got Jesus crucified. He went on to explain that Jesus had risen from the dead and had now sent his Holy Spirit to fill his followers and give them power to tell people this great news. As this disciple – who was called Peter - spoke, Isaac and Anna were transfixed along with so many others. Peter went on to explain how Jesus had died, but it was God's plan - that he would die so people could be forgiven for all of their sin. He testified to the crowd that God had raised Jesus from the dead because he had paid the price for their sin and now, they could get to know God as their Father who loved them very much.

Isaac and Anna could not believe their ears at what they were hearing, nor their eyes at what they were seeing, when people all around them began to fall to their knees; some were weeping, some laughing, a lot of them were shaking, but all were asking Jesus to forgive them.

"What on earth is happening?" asked Anna as she watched grown men crying like babies.

Suddenly, Isaac knew in his heart, that everything that Anna had told him about Jesus, everything that he had just heard Peter say, was all true! He turned to tell Anna that he finally believed, when he recognised the two slave traders fighting their way towards them! He gasped in horror and pulled Anna away back through the crowds.

"No Isaac, I need to stay!" sobbed Anna, tears streaming down her cheeks, "I believe him! He's telling the truth, I knew it! Jesus is alive!"

"I know, I know! I believe too, but we have to leave right now, trust me!"

Anna resisted and tried to pull away as Isaac screamed at her, "Anna, please, now!"

Isaac pulled Anna with all his strength and managed to drag her away from the crowd and down into a side alley. He pushed her against the wall and put his hand over her mouth as she started to protest. Anna looked into Isaac's eyes and saw terror; she suddenly realised that something must have been very wrong for Isaac to behave in such a way! The same old fear that she had felt all that time ago hiding behind the blanket in Mary's house, came flooding back.

The children stayed pressed against the wall as quietly as they could. Isaac held his breath, hoping against hope that the two men had not seen them go into the alleyway. Anna was both confused and petrified; why did they suddenly have to hide? What had so terrified Isaac? She looked at Isaac pleadingly, but he just shook his head with his hand still over her mouth.

Then as two men come around the corner and started to walk towards her and Isaac with huge menacing grins on their faces, sudden realisation hit Anna like a chariot at full speed. She recognised those men. One of them raised an arm; the hand was missing!

Isaac backed away pulling Anna with him, but he had managed to lead them into a dead end, and he realised too late that there was no escape!

"Well, well, well! What have we here? Two for the price of one!" Anna remembered the rough voice that she had heard as she hid in Mary's house. The children froze in fear.

"It's taken a long time to find you, girl, but the wait's been worthwhile now we have your friend as well. With the two of you, I'll get my revenge and make some money!"

The smaller man with the scar leered at them both as he pulled out two sets of manacles.

"No!" screamed Anna as the men grabbed her and Isaac. Both children fought as hard as they could with fists and feet, but it was useless. They were no match for these two bear-like captors! Despite only having one hand, the man's grip on Anna was vice-like. She reached up to scratch his face with her free hand, but he leaned back out of her reach and struck her a glancing blow on the side of her head with his mutilated arm. Stunned, Anna barely noticed as they were shackled and taken away.

Isaac had lost all sense of direction and had no idea where they were being taken. He hoped someone would notice, but either no-one saw, or no-one cared. They were carried for a while, Isaac struggling all the way and desperately scared for Anna who did not seem to be moving at all. They came to a house, one among many. Isaac could see nothing to distinguish this from any of the surrounding buildings, which would make it all the harder to come back and rescue Anna even if somehow he managed to escape himself.

The men opened the heavy wooden door of the house and roughly dragged the children in. Isaac fought as hard as he could and even tried to bite one of the men as a gag was forced into his mouth. He was rewarded with a hefty slap across his face, and he tasted his own blood.

Having successfully gagged the shackled children, the men pulled aside a rug on the floor to reveal a wooden trapdoor; Isaac's eyes widened in fear, he was glad that Anna was still a little dazed at this point and did not seem to notice. The man with the scar lifted the trapdoor to reveal some steps leading down to a dark, damp cellar.

Isaac struggled as he was picked up and taken to the top of the steps leading down to the cellar. The man with the scar cuffed Isaac again, "There's no point fighting, you could make as much noise as you want down there, no-one's going to hear you!" and he roughly pushed Isaac down the steps.

Anna was still dazed, and unaware of what was happening to her, as 'Scar-face' dragged her down the steps. She did not even notice when her leg caught on the door hinge on the way down leaving a nasty gash.

The trapdoor was slammed shut and bolted and the children were left alone in the darkness. Isaac was beside himself, as he and Anna lay on the floor. He tried desperately to get to his feet, but his head was spinning and his legs felt shaky, and he could not stand up. He resorted to wriggling his way closer to Anna to see if she was okay. Gagged, he could do no more than grunt at Anna. He was more scared than he had ever been in his life! Anna seemed dazed and he was terrified that she was badly injured. It was all his fault; he went down the wrong alley! He should have taken more care of Anna and now he was helpless, there was nothing he could do. Tears of frustration and fear ran down his cheek, "Jesus, I believe in you, I'm sorry I didn't believe before, but I need you now! Please get us out of this," he thought desperately.

A few moments later, Anna came out of her daze and her eyes widened in fear as she took in her surroundings. She felt Isaac's hands take hers and after a few moments as her eyes adjusted to the darkness, she could make out his face and see that he was gagged as she was. She too called out to Jesus in her head, "Help us!"

Isaac's head slowly stopped spinning and his legs felt steadier so, letting go of Anna's hands, he struggled to his knees and crawled awkwardly back to the cellar steps. He worked his way up the steps careful not to make a sound. Reaching up to the trapdoor, he pushed against it as hard as he could without success. The heavy trapdoor was firmly bolted shut.

For Simeon and Lydia, the morning had started in much the same way as every other morning, except that they had risen earlier than usual. Simeon, hoping to sell extra bread now that there were so many more people in the city for the special feast, rose first.

Lydia followed shortly afterwards and began to milk the goats.

While he baked, Simeon was thinking about a conversation he had had a few days before with two men who had come to the bakery late in the day when he was not terribly busy.

The conversation had turned to the amount of bread Simeon had to bake with his growing business – his bread was extremely popular, and Simeon took pride in the comments he got from many people saying he baked the best bread in the city.

But he was worn out, he worked so hard, as did Lydia, and the growing demand was taking its toll on them both. He had decided that he needed some helpers.

"I think I need to find a couple of youngsters to do a bit of work," he had grudgingly admitted to the two men.

"We might be able to help you out there, we're hoping to acquire a young girl soon, we could sell her to you," one of the men had said.

At first Simeon was uncertain about the prospect, he knew all about slave traders and their business, after all slavery was common practise; but he was unsure how Lydia would feel about owning a slave. Simeon was rich; he did not really need to work at all, but he was greedy and did not want to spend his huge inheritance. He could have afforded many servants to help. He and Lydia could have lived a life of luxury if they had chosen to, but they both liked to work hard, it was a good distraction from the misery of their marriage.

In the end Simeon's desire to increase his business and make more money triumphed over any concerns that his wife might voice. After some fierce haggling, they agreed a price and arranged to meet again once the men had acquired the girl. Simeon decided Lydia would never need to know all the details of this transaction, in fact, the less she knew, the better!

Lydia interrupted his thoughts, "I'm just going to fetch water."

He nodded and sighed as he watched his wife trudge wearily from the house. He had thought their married life would be very different, but he could not give her what she yearned for the most, a child of her own.

When Lydia returned, she and Simeon worked together in silence until it was time for Lydia to leave for her daily trip to the market.

The door to the bakery crashed open and Simeon looked up in surprise as Lydia came rushing back in having only just left! She was out of breath, her eyes glistening, "Simeon, come quickly! There's something going on, come and see!"

"What is it woman?" he growled sullenly.

"Just come with me!" said Lydia.

Simeon followed her reluctantly, knowing he had time before the next batch of dough could go in the oven.

They came to a crowd of people in the square, there was all sorts of noise going on; they heard men speaking in strange languages, they heard some people making fun of them, others trying to quieten them so they could listen. Simeon, being a large man, was able to push his way to the front of the crowd and Lydia followed in his wake. There was a group of men and women, some laughing, some crying, some even shaking, in various states of disarray, speaking in these strange languages. One of the men stepped forward and stood apart from the others and raised his voice. A hush came over the crowd as the man spoke, "This is what was spoken of by the prophet Joel..." the man went on to explain that God was pouring out his Spirit, then he talked about Jesus.

Simeon had heard about Jesus, heard about the miracles, how he had been crucified and the rumours about his rising from the dead, but he had never heard anyone speak like this before. He wanted to get away from this man who was making him feel so uncomfortable, but he could not bring himself to leave.

His eyes were riveted on this man. There was nothing about his appearance that was special, in fact he looked completely ordinary. But the way he spoke! It was as though Simeon was the only person in the crowd, as though the man was speaking directly to him. The man spoke like he knew God, not knew about him, but actually knew him.

For some reason, Simeon's mind went back to his own childhood when his father had taken him to the temple to show him where he worked. Simeon was just eight years old and remembered watching an old man walk up to a young couple who had brought their tiny baby to the temple. The old man took the baby in his arms and spoke loudly enough for Simeon to hear as he was standing so close, "My eyes have now seen God's Messiah sent to save mankind, I can now die in peace," the old man had said. Simeon had always remembered this old man because they shared the same name.

He had asked his father what the old Simeon had meant, but his father had brushed him off saying the old man was talking nonsense due to his advanced years. When Anna, a well-known prophetess who was respected by those in the temple, also began to say something similar, his father had become even more uncomfortable and whisked Simeon away before he could hear any more. But that memory had stayed with him. Was this Jesus the one that the old man and Anna had talked about? Was this Jesus God's Messiah sent to save mankind?

Simeon continued to listen and as he did so it seemed like a heavy fog began to lift from his eyes and he could see clearly for the first-time in... well, ever! He began to believe that what he had witnessed in the temple all those years ago was the truth. That what this man, a disciple of Jesus, was saying, was true!

Simeon found himself on his knees as he called out to Jesus. He came to the realisation, this Jesus who had been crucified was the Messiah that God had promised, the one the Jews had been waiting for, for a very long time. Simeon wept as he asked God to forgive him, and confessed that he believed in Jesus, believed that Jesus was God's son, his saviour. Simeon's hard and bitter heart melted as he experienced God loving him right there and then in that moment. He heard the man speak about being born again and turned to Lydia to tell her that this was exactly what it felt like for him, that he had been given a new heart; but as he turned, he saw she was also on her knees, crying and asking for forgiveness as were many others all around them.

Simeon and Lydia stayed where they were for several hours. The dough, waiting to go in the oven, was forgotten. All around them people were embracing one another, laughing, crying, calling out to Jesus, their hearts being filled with love, joy and peace by God's Holy Spirit. Hundreds of people also did what Simeon had done; they believed what had been said, they believed in Jesus and asked him for forgiveness.

It was late evening before Simeon and Lydia walked home, hand in hand, and talked about the day. They laughed when they saw the ruined dough.

"Just this morning I would have been angry at the waste of money!" said Simeon as he threw the useless dough away, "But what happened to us today is worth so much more! Oh Lydia, I've been so wrong! I was so angry with God, I blamed him for everything that went wrong in my life. I never knew how much he really loved me! Lydia, I'm sorry, can you forgive me for being so angry and distant?"

Lydia embraced Simeon, "I forgive you and I'm sorry, I too have blamed God and been angry with him, but now I feel so different!" she said, "Oh Simeon, I feel so hopeful, it's like all my pain at being childless has gone and now I feel so comforted and loved by Jesus, by God. I am so grateful; I can't express it.... I have no words" Lydia wept tears of joy, relief, and gratitude.

"I know, love," Simeon wrapped his arms around her and, looking into her eyes, saw a new life.

Over the next few days, Simeon and Lydia made many new friends with other people who had also had their lives changed on that special day. They spent a lot of time in each other's houses, eating together, worshipping, praying together, sometimes meeting with Peter and John and the other apostles in various places where they would spend hours listening to the apostles' stories about Jesus.

Simeon's bakery business took second place, as his priorities changed from simply making money to spending time getting to know the God that he had been taught about as a Jewish child.

Late one evening, Simeon and Lydia were coming back from spending time with some of their newfound friends, when they stopped short as they saw two men waiting at their door. Simeon's face fell as he recognised them, "Oh Lydia, I had forgotten."

"What is it?" Lydia was concerned at the look on Simeon's face, but got no answer as the men noticed them and walked towards them.

"We've got her, and another one; a boy if you want him, they'll be good workers," one of the men said, getting straight to the point.

"I'm sorry," replied Simeon, "you've had a wasted journey, so much has changed, I can't own any slaves!"

Lydia looked shocked, "What's going on?"

"We had a deal!" the men looked angry.

"Simeon?" Lydia asked again.

Simeon turned to Lydia, "Forgive me, I spoke to these men a while ago about getting extra help around here and I agreed to buy a slave girl, but I can't do it, not now."

Simeon's expression turned to complete shock as he heard Lydia say, "You must. Buy them both. Simeon do it!"

Simeon's mouth moved but no words came out. Surely Lydia did not approve of slavery? But then he had the strangest sensation that he should do what Lydia was asking, as if another voice said, "Do it," and as he decided to obey that voice, a wonderful sense of peace filled his heart, and he knew it was the right thing to do. Simeon later realised that it was the Holy Spirit who had come to live in his heart who was urging him to rescue these two children.

"Okay," he said to the two men, "but tell me you didn't steal them from their parents."

"They're both orphans. The girl's father owed me a lot of money when he was killed, so er... by rights I own her. And the boy – well he'll be better off as a slave. Trust me, I'm doing them both a kindness, they're lucky to have survived this long on the streets, it's a harsh life."

Simeon wasn't sure if he believed the men's story, but he quickly agreed a price for both children. The men said they would be back within the hour.

Once inside their house, Simeon looked at Lydia, "I know it's a terrible thing to do, to buy people"

"Yes, it is Simeon, but see how God has turned it around, what you meant for evil he has turned to good! They can become our children;

we can give them a home and love them as if they were our own flesh and blood!"

Simeon was taken aback, "W... what?" he stammered.

"Think about it, Simeon, what would you do with them? We would never treat them as slaves, we couldn't let them go back out on the streets. You know we've wanted children for a long time!"

"But our own children! Not someone else's!" protested Simeon.

"They will be ours! We can grow to love them; I know we can! What if this has been God's plan all along? That we would look after these orphans? Simeon please!" begged Lydia.

Simeon was in shock! Normally adopting orphans was not something he would ever have considered doing, but everything had changed so much; his ordinary life had recently become extraordinary! He was no longer sure what 'normal' life was meant to look like! He looked into Lydia's pleading eyes and knew that he would do whatever he could to give her what she had always wanted, "Okay, let's see how it goes."

For Lydia, that was all she needed to hear, she was confident that he would come round to her proposal in time.

Simeon smiled at his wife, he loved the difference in her, it was like a shadow had lifted from her heart.

"It'll be alright!" Lydia reassured him.

They hugged for a long time until Lydia broke away and gasped, "We have to get them mattresses to sleep on! And clothes!"

Simeon laughed, "Relax Lydia, most of that will have to wait until tomorrow. I would imagine those poor children will be grateful to sleep on a floor if it's indoors and safe!"

Isaac and Anna had been locked up in the dark, damp cellar for a few days. After the first day, their gags had been removed. They had tried shouting on and off, but had given up, when it became clear no-one could hear them. Isaac had persuaded the men to unshackle their hands so they could more easily eat and drink the stale water and bits of bread that were brought them at different times. The children had tried in vain to open the cellar door and explored every inch of the cellar walls to try and find a means of escape, but to no avail. They had at least been given a blanket to sleep under. From the snippets of conversation they had heard, it seemed that the men were looking for someone but every time they went to this person's house, they were not in. The men were becoming more and more bad-tempered until late one night they came back in a much better mood. They unlocked the cellar door and carried the children up the steps. Isaac and Anna blinked as their eyes adjusted from the dark cellar to the lamplit room.

Anna was trembling, she was not sure if it was from fear or cold or both. As soon as she was put down, Anna edged closer to Isaac, cowering next to him. He took hold of her hand, trying to reassure her. The men put gags back on them and warned them on pain of death not to try anything foolish like running away.

The man with no hand smiled at Anna, but it was more like a sneer than a happy smile, "Well, you'll be pleased to know that your father's debt is about to be paid off!"

Anna was petrified. This could only mean one thing; that they had found a buyer for her and maybe Isaac too.

"We're taking you to your new owner, there's no point in screaming, or trying to escape, because once the money's paid, they own you... and they can do whatever they like with you."

The children found themselves being gripped tightly around the arms and dragged out of the house, down one alleyway after another. They struggled, but the men were so much stronger, it was pointless. They had no idea where they were going as it was dark. After a while, Isaac thought he knew where they were but was unable to communicate with Anna.

It was not long before Anna too realised where they were. Dread filled her and she felt sick as she realised that they had arrived at the house of 'Angry Eyes' the baker.

"No!" Anna screamed in her head as she struggled as hard as she could. She looked at Isaac with wide, terrified eyes.

The men took the gags off the children warning them to keep quiet. Anna was so terrified; she did not say a word.

Trembling, Anna edged closer to Isaac. He squeezed her hand doing his best to convey without words that he would look after her. Right now, Isaac felt angry more than anything else, and decided, that whatever happened, he would somehow find a way to get out of this.

The door of the house next to the bakery opened, and the children were roughly pushed inside. 'Angry Eyes' silently handed the men some money and they left without a backward glance.

Anna noticed that the men had left the door slightly open, and she edged slowly towards it. Inside, the house was quite dark as it was only lit by one small lamp.

Anna looked around and for the first time noticed 'Mrs Angry Eyes' in the corner of the room. For a moment, 'Angry Eyes' himself turned away from the children towards his wife and Anna made a split-second decision to run for it, hoping Isaac would follow. She darted out of the door, just ducking underneath the arms of 'Angry Eyes' as he moved to grab her, and ran as fast as she could!

Isaac tried to follow, but 'Angry Eyes' caught him.

"Let go of me!" yelled Isaac. "I won't stay here!" He struggled as hard as he could and even managed to bite Angry Eyes' hand that was gripping his wrist, but the man did not let go.

"Aaargh! Child! Stop. Please!" surprisingly, 'Angry Eyes' voice was calm. It was nothing like Isaac remembered and he was a little taken aback. Isaac looked straight at 'Angry Eyes' and saw that something had changed. This was not the man who had chased them away from the bakery, was it? Isaac was puzzled. This man looked the same yet somehow seemed totally different.

"I'm not going to hurt you, please give me a chance to explain," said Simeon, shutting the door after checking to see if he could see the girl anywhere at all. He let Isaac go as Lydia lit another couple of lamps, "we will have to try and find your friend as soon as possible, but she could be anywhere by now."

"Well, I'm not helping you!" said Isaac stubbornly.

"What's your name?" asked Lydia, speaking for the first time since Isaac's arrival.

Isaac looked at her but did not answer. She spoke again, "I'm really sorry about what you've been through, you must have been so scared." Isaac noticed that she had tears in her eyes, like she was pleading with him. He was so confused, what was happening?

"Lad, we are not going to hurt you. Yes, we bought you, but only to free you from the slave traders. I'm asking you to hear me out and then if you don't want to stay, you are free to go, I promise," Simeon explained.

"Please, sit down," said Lydia, and Isaac noticed it was definitely a request, not a demand.

Isaac cautiously perched on a wooden stool that was placed on one side of a large wooden table and folded his arms defensively. Simeon and Lydia sat opposite him, and Simeon spoke, "I recognise you, lad, you've taken some of my bread before, haven't you?"

"Here it comes!" thought Isaac, suddenly afraid, waiting for the beating that was sure to come his way.

Simeon noticed straight away how the boy flinched in fear and he held up his hands, saying, "I won't hurt you, I'm sorry I was so angry with you back then, but I'm a different person now." It grieved Simeon to see this child so scared of him. Only a few days ago he would have been glad, but now that his heart had been changed by Jesus, it saddened him.

"My name is Simeon," he said, "and this is my wife, Lydia. What's your name?" Isaac was asked again.

Isaac sat tight lipped, refusing to answer.

Simeon continued, "That's okay, you can tell us later. Have you heard about Jesus?"

Isaac had planned to say nothing at all, but he could not help himself replying as the conversation took this unexpected turn, "Yes," he said simply.

"Good. Well, we encountered Jesus on the Day of the Feast, and he changed our hearts. I was not a very nice person, but being loved and forgiven by Jesus has totally changed me, and Lydia."

"It's true," said Lydia.

Isaac looked at his new "owners" with suspicion. He desperately wanted to believe what this man was saying, and he could see that he looked different from how he had remembered him. He knew it was not outside the realms of possibility that he was telling the truth because he and Anna had seen what had happened to other people on the Day of the Feast. But they had also seen this man angry before. Could Isaac trust what he was being told?

As Simeon and Lydia continued to share their hearts, Isaac began to relax just a little. He looked into their eyes. There was a noticeable difference in them. Dare he believe them?

Simeon and Lydia had stopped talking and looked at Isaac expectantly, waiting for him to say something, but he did not know what to say. In that instant, Isaac somehow felt reassured that they were telling the truth. He remembered how he himself had suddenly believed in Jesus on that same day. Isaac felt a huge wave of emotion, and he tried desperately to stop himself crying with relief. He angrily brushed a tear away. Boys do not cry! But it was a lost cause when Lydia got up, walked around the table, took him in her arms and held him just as his own mother had once done. He tried to resist at first but then could fight it no longer. All the months of trying to be brave, looking after Anna, pushing down the fear that at times had almost engulfed him, had taken their toll. He sobbed as he realised that Jesus had answered his prayer and rescued him by bringing him to this couple who had been transformed by their experience of God's love. Isaac's doubt subsided, he knew in his heart that he was safe, and that Jesus was alive and had answered his prayer.

Suddenly he pulled himself away, "What about Anna?" he sniffed as he wiped away his tears.

"Is that the name of the little girl who was with you?" asked Lydia.

Isaac nodded. "Yes, but she's not used to being on her own, I've been looking after her, she'll be so scared! She will get lost; she doesn't know the city like I do!" Isaac felt panic starting to rise.

Simeon, who had come round to Isaac's side of the table, placed his hand on Isaac's shoulder, "Don't worry lad, I'm sure we'll find her. You and I will go out looking tonight and again tomorrow and the next day and every day after that until we do. Now, before we go, you haven't told us your name yet..."

"Isaac."

"Well, that's a great name, Isaac. You need to have something to eat and drink first, then we'll go and look for Anna."

Chapter eight

Fire

Anna had run as fast as her legs would carry her! She ran through alley-way after alleyway, turning left then right as much as she could to make it harder for anyone who might be chasing her to find her. She stopped; panting, sweating, and gasping for air when she came across a stack of old baskets that she could hide behind. Her frantic dash through the alleyways had caused the gash on her leg that had started to heal, to open up again and she wiped away the blood that was trickling down her leg with the corner of her filthy tunic.

She was terrified; what had happened to Isaac? She did not know if he had got away. He was faster than her, so surely, he would have caught up with her. Unless he had not seen which way she went. Or maybe he did not get away, in which case she would need to go back and try to rescue him somehow! She was on her own, she had no idea where she was, how would she find her way back to rescue Isaac? She tried to calm herself down, what should she do now? More than at any other time in the last couple of months she suddenly missed Mary.

Mary would have known what to do. Anna could not help herself; she began to sob in utter despair.

Tired, hungry, and alone, Anna decided she would have to stay where she was and try and find the bakery again in the morning when it was light, she would have no chance now in the dark. Maybe then she could rescue Isaac. Exhausted, she curled up into a ball and drifted off into an uneasy sleep hidden behind the baskets.

As soon as it was light the next day, Anna knew she had to move. As she got up from the ground, she noticed that her leg was feeling stiff and sore. She looked down and saw that the cut on her leg had become red and hot to the touch, crusted with dried blood.

Limping, Anna made her way warily through the alleyways trying to find the bazaar so that she could get her bearings. She knew that now it was daylight she had a better chance of finding out where she was. She realised that she had always relied on Isaac to guide them each day. Turning a corner, she saw the bazaar, "Ah, now I know," she said to herself, "I know where I am. But where to now? How do I get to the bakery?"

Anna looked around, she was starving, having eaten next to nothing the day before, "Come on, Anna," she spoke to herself, "you have to beg for some money! Why did you always leave that up to Isaac?"

After two hours of unsuccessful begging where everyone either ignored her pleas, or pretended not to see her at all, she muttered to herself, "Now I know why I always left it to Isaac!"

Anna fought back the tears and the panic, realising this was the first time she had been without Isaac for an awfully long time. Stomach rumbling, Anna just did not know what to do, "I don't know how to get to the bakery! What if Isaac escaped and he's not there? How will I find him? Where should I go?" she said to herself. Then she remembered the place that she and Isaac agreed they would meet if they ever got separated, "Of course! The stable up on the hill with the straw in it! That's where we agreed to meet."

Anna knew it would take her at least an hour to get to the stable, so she set off at a run which quickly turned into a slow limp as her leg became increasingly painful. She tried to ignore it as she limped on towards the stable, hoping against hope that Isaac would have escaped and found his way there. She eventually arrived two hours later and rushed through the doorway. All her hopes were dashed to the ground when she saw that she was alone; Isaac was not there.

Anna lay down on the straw feeling exhausted and in pain. Her leg had swollen even more and was red and hot. She knew that was not good, but felt too sore and unwell to do anything about it. Even though it was the middle of the day, she fell into an uneasy sleep.

She woke up just as it was starting to get dark. Desperately thirsty but no longer hungry, she tried to get up, but fell back down again as her head started to spin. Feeling sick and dizzy, she stayed where she was and once again fell into a feverish sleep.

That first night, Simeon and Isaac had searched the streets and alleyways around the bakery for hours for Anna but without success. Isaac had remembered about the old stable where he and Anna were supposed to meet if they got separated, but he knew she would not be able to leave the city after nightfall as the gates would be closed and guarded. When Simeon noticed that Isaac was so tired he could barely stand, he insisted that they went home. They would try again in the morning. Isaac protested but Simeon was firm, "We will find her, Isaac, she's probably hiding really well somewhere right now. It'll be easier in the daylight."

"She won't manage on her own," yawned Isaac, "what if those men kidnap her again?"

"They won't, don't forget, I've bought her, she belongs to us now. Come on, Isaac, let's go back. Look, I don't know very much about Jesus, but I do know that he looks after people. We need to trust him that he loves Anna and will protect her."

"She always believed in him you know, even when I didn't," said Isaac.

"I'm looking forward to getting to know her," replied Simeon taking Isaac's hand to help him along.

When they arrived home, Lydia was waiting, "You couldn't find her?" she asked, knowing the answer.

Simeon shook his head as he sat down wearily, Isaac beside him, "We'll look again tomorrow."

"Poor lad, he's dead on his feet," said Lydia, looking at Isaac who had finally given in and was fast asleep, his head resting on his hands on the table, "I've borrowed a mattress from a neighbour and made up a bed for him."

Simeon picked Isaac up, appalled at how little he weighed and carried him upstairs.

"Poor child," whispered Lydia following behind Simeon, "do you think we will find Anna?"

"We have to, this lad won't rest until he finds her, and neither will I!" Both Simeon and Lydia were exhausted but their heads were buzzing with what had happened over the last few days. Their lives had been turned upside down, "We had better go to bed," yawned Simeon, "come on," he put his arm around his wife, "don't worry, it'll all work out."

The next morning Isaac awoke and at first was totally confused about his surroundings and was stunned to find himself sleeping on a mattress! No wonder he had slept so deeply. He was about to say something to Anna when he suddenly remembered everything that had happened.

He sat up quickly, "I have to find Anna!" he said aloud to the empty room.

Isaac sprang up from the mattress and looked around. He had not seen this room yesterday. Was he still in Simeon and Lydia's house? Where were they? He saw a large piece of linen draped across the middle of the room. Curiously, he crept over to it and peeked around it.

There was a bed, a large wooden bed, not just a mattress! He assumed it belonged to Simeon and Lydia, but they were no longer in it. He turned back towards his mattress and the doorway, there were some stairs going down on the inside of the house, and he realised that for the first time in his life he was in a house with a second storey. Not only that, but the stairs were also on the inside, which was very unusual!

Isaac cautiously walked down the stairs. As he neared the bottom step, he could hear Simeon talking in a hushed voice. He moved into the room, recognising it as the kitchen he had been in the night before. Simeon and Lydia were sitting at the table, they looked up.

Before they even had a chance to greet Isaac, he said, "I have to find Anna! I have to go now and find her!"

"Hold on Isaac! Slow down! Sit and eat first, then we'll search," said Simeon.

Isaac sat on a stool and helped himself to some goat's milk and delicious freshly baked bread that Simeon had made that morning. He ate and drank as fast as he could, desperate to begin the search but also enjoying his breakfast.

"There's a place we need to go to this morning," Isaac said in between mouthfuls of bread, "there's a stable up on the hill outside the city where Anna and I agreed to meet if we ever got separated. I'm hoping she's remembered to go there, and found her way." he said, wiping goat's milk from his chin.

It was still early in the morning when they left the city and made their way up to the stable. Isaac eagerly ran up the hill and burst through the doorway of the old derelict building. He was filled with disappointment as he realised that the place was empty, Anna was nowhere to be seen. Unbeknown to them, at that very moment Anna was begging for food very unsuccessfully in the bazaar, not far from the bakery.

They waited for an hour to see if Anna would turn up, but Isaac was impatient and wanted to return to the city to search all the other places he and Anna used to visit together. But they could not find her, as unfortunately, Anna had left by a different gate just after they had returned to the city. After another fruitless search, Isaac wearily trudged home with Simeon, his worry for Anna growing.

As they approached the bakery, Simeon realised that this was the first time in many years that he had left Lydia to do all the baking, but he knew his wife did not mind the extra work. God had done a miracle in their hearts because right now, all they cared about was finding this poor defenceless child. He looked at Isaac and wondered how he had managed to survive all on his own and look after Anna, but there would be time to find out Isaac's story once they had found her.

That evening, frustrated with their lack of success in finding Anna, Simeon, Lydia, and Isaac sat down to eat. Simeon had to insist that Isaac went to bed after dinner otherwise he would have gone out again that night to continue the search. Lydia went upstairs with him and tried to reassure him.

"I won't be able to sleep!" insisted Isaac.

Lydia stroked Isaac's forehead and brushed his long hair out of his eyes. "Shall we pray?" she asked.

Isaac did not know what to say, he had never prayed with anyone before. He had repeated prayers that his mother had taught him, but after recent events he had a feeling that praying was going to be very different, "I don't know how to."

"Neither do I really, I'm new to all this too!" smiled Lydia, "Perhaps we could learn together, it's just having a conversation with God, after all."

They simply poured their hearts out to Jesus and told him all their worries about Anna, asking earnestly for him to keep her safe. After just a few moments, Isaac began to feel sleepy; he did not even notice when Lydia crept out of the room.

Meanwhile, Anna was having an altogether different type of night. The cut on her leg had become infected and as the infection seeped into her blood and spread around her body, she had become delirious.

Whilst in this fevered state, she dreamt:

She was running hard, away from a fire that was catching up with her. She screamed out for Isaac, but she could not see him. Then she heard his voice telling her to turn around and run down an alleyway. She did so, and then she saw him. Isaac took hold of her hand and they ran together with the fire lapping hungrily at their heels. Just in time, Isaac led her to the end of the alleyway and out into a field. She turned around to speak to Isaac, but he was gone, as was the alleyway. Confused, Anna turned back and saw Jesus sitting by a stream under a tree. There was no one else around, it was peaceful and quiet, and the fire was gone. He turned his head to look at her, a huge grin on his face. He patted the ground next to him, "Hi Anna, come and sit with me."

She did not need asking twice, even in a dream! Anna settled herself down next to Jesus and looked up into his face. She loved his face, those wonderful eyes! So penetrating, so full of love. She felt safe. Anna had never felt so happy, so complete. She could have sat there with Jesus forever - at that moment in time, nothing else mattered. She just wanted to be with him, she never wanted to leave his side.

"I've known you for a very long time, Anna," said Jesus.

"Since that first time I saw you when I was with my dad?" she asked.

"Long before that."

"My dad died."

"I know."

"I had to run away."

"I know that too."

"How do you know?"

"I came with you."

"I didn't see you."

"But you felt me."

Anna smiled, "I think sometimes I did, but most of the time I was scared, and to be honest, I thought you couldn't hear me!"

"I've always been with you, Anna. Look!" said Jesus, and he showed her, it was like she was watching herself over the past few months.

First, she saw Mary. Jesus was whispering in Mary's ear. Mary nodded and hid Anna behind the embroidered blanket in her house.

Then she saw Zechariah. Mary was talking to him, and Jesus whispered in his ear and he agreed to take Anna to Jerusalem.

Then there was what Anna could only describe as an angel at the well giving her the goatskin. At this point Anna interrupted, "Wait, that wasn't an angel, it was a woman at the well!"

"Was it?" asked Jesus.

He continued to show her: There was Isaac, Jesus whispered in his ear and pointed to Anna sitting on the steps.

She watched as Jesus asked the kind stallholder to feed her and Isaac.

And so, it went on; many things Anna had not even been aware of.

He showed her angels watching over her and Isaac everywhere they slept. She saw Jesus divert the slave traders away from them. Anna gasped, "But it didn't work, they found us!"

"I know."

"So how is this good?" Anna asked worriedly.

"You'll see," Jesus smiled down at her, "Trust me, Anna." And then, everything went misty.

The next morning Isaac woke up with a start. He had had a dream, and in it, Anna was sitting in their stable, saying to him, "You told me to come here if we got separated; I'm here now, I need your help, come and get me!"

He sprang out of bed and judging by the gentle snoring coming from the other side of the linen, realised it was probably still early. But Isaac did not care. Even if Simeon got cross with him, it did not matter, he knew without a doubt that Anna was at the stable at last! He shouted at Simeon and Lydia, "Wake up! I know where she is, I had a dream, she's at our special place, she wasn't there yesterday but I know she is now!"

He raced downstairs without waiting for them, about to run out into the streets when Simeon, hurrying down the stairs, called after him, "Wait, Isaac! I'm coming!"

"I know where she is!" yelled Isaac, "We have to go now!"

"Just a moment Isaac! Calm down!" said Simeon rubbing his eyes. He was used to getting up early but at a much slower pace!

"I had a dream. Anna spoke to me in the dream and said she was at our stable! We have to go now!" gabbled Isaac urgently.

"She wasn't there yesterday when you looked..." began Lydia who had followed Simeon down the stairs.

"But she is now, I know it! We have to go now!" Isaac was desperate for them to understand his hurry.

"And we will go; but let us have breakfast first," said Simeon stretching and yawning.

"Right, I'll make us some breakfast," said Lydia.

"I don't want breakfast. I just need to go and get Anna, I think she's in trouble!" pleaded Isaac.

"Ok Isaac, we'll grab some food and take it with us," said Simeon, seeing Isaac's desperation.

Lydia gave them some leftover bread from the day before as they walked towards the door. Isaac stopped suddenly, "Wait, I have to go on my own," he said.

Lydia looked at him sharply, "What?"

"I have to go on my own to find Anna, if she sees either of you, she'll likely run away, she doesn't know you aren't 'Mr and Mrs Angry Eyes' anymore," Isaac clamped his hand over his mouth, his eyes wide with fear when he realised what he had called them.

He shied away when Simeon raised his hand, expecting a blow, but Simeon just rested his hand on his arm and reassured him, "It's okay Isaac. That's actually a rather good description of us!" he laughed.

"Not anymore!" smiled Lydia "I still can't believe what's happened to us, I feel like a whole new person!"

Isaac could not believe it either, that he was in the same house as 'Mr and Mrs Angry Eyes', that he had sat at their table and eaten with them!

"Okay," said Simeon, "I will come with you as far as I can without Anna seeing me, then you go up to your hiding place and see if she's there."

"I'm coming too," said Lydia.

"You don't need to," said Simeon, "we'll manage."

"Yes, I do, she may need me, I want to be there for her, and we still have time before I need to start baking, and if it's a little late today, people will just have to wait for their bread, this is important!"

Simeon squeezed her hand.

The three of them set off together like a little family. Lydia watched Isaac, and saw a boy trying desperately to be a man and she longed to comfort him and be a mother to him.

Already she had felt love growing in her heart for this boy and the girl she was yet to know. A little while after they had left the city through one of the gates, Isaac came to a halt, "I think you had better wait here and stay out of sight. Any further and she might see you."

"Ok Isaac, we'll wait, we're not going anywhere," reassured Simeon.

Isaac set off on his own and ran up the familiar path leading to the old stable. His heart was thumping when he arrived, not just from the exertion of running up the hill, but in anticipation – would she be there? Had she remembered? He hesitated before he went in, took a deep breath, and stepped inside. At first, he thought she was not there, and disappointment washed over him, but then he saw her curled up in the corner! Tears of relief flowed down his cheeks. He saw she was asleep, so he stepped towards her.

"Anna, I'm here, I came yesterday..." he began to explain, but he stopped short when he saw her close up. She did not look well.

He shook her arm, "Wake up Anna!" he cried. But she would not wake. Her forehead was burning hot and he realised she had a fever. Her breaths were shallow, and he noticed her leg was cut and swollen. For a moment, Isaac froze in terror not knowing what to do. Was she going to die? In desperation he called out, "Jesus, please! Do something, make her better! What should I do?"

Isaac realised he needed to get back to Simeon and Lydia for help because even though Anna was small, he could not carry her. He did not want to leave her either, he was so afraid for her. "Jesus," he said, "please take care of Anna, while I go and get some help."

Reluctantly, he backed out of the stable, unable to drag his eyes away from his best friend who looked so small and vulnerable. It was one of the hardest things he had ever had to do, but he knew he needed to get

Simeon and Lydia as quickly as possible. He turned and ran back down the hill.

Seeing Isaac racing down the hill towards them, Simeon and Lydia came rushing up the hill to meet him, "Is she not there?" asked Lydia, but then she saw Isaac's face and the tears streaming down his cheeks.

Isaac words were incomprehensible as he tried to tell them how he had found Anna.

"Isaac, lad, you need to calm down!" Simeon took hold of Isaac, "Look at me, take a breath. Talk to me."

"She's... she's ill, hurt, so hot, I think it's her leg, I can't wake her up!"

Simeon immediately let go of Isaac and started to run up the hill followed more slowly by Lydia and a panting Isaac.

When he got to the ruined building, Simeon went inside and at first saw no-one until he realised that the bundle of rags lying on the ground in the corner of the stable was a child.

"Anna!" he cried out as he picked her up in his arms. It felt like she weighed less than a basket of bread! He looked at her and knew instantly that she was gravely ill, her tunic was soaked with sweat, she was feverish, and hardly breathing. He saw her red, swollen leg and remembered an uncle of his who had a wound that got infected; he had refused to get any medical help and a few days later he had died as the infection had spread around his body. Simeon prayed that it was not too late for Anna!

"It's her leg, it's infected and it's made her ill. We need to get her home," he said as the other two arrived. Isaac followed anxiously as Simeon carried Anna. He kept looking at Anna willing her to wake up.

"Simeon, I don't think there's anything we can do! The infection has already taken hold!" sobbed Lydia.

"Look over there! That crowd of people, isn't that Peter talking to them? Yes, it is, come on!" Isaac brightened up, following Simeon at a run,

"Yes! Jesus used to heal people! I know he could do it, but can his disciples?"

As he got to the crowd of people listening to Peter, Simeon recognised the apostle John off to one side, talking to a smaller group. He headed for John and unapologetically pushed his way through the small group of people and interrupted John as he was speaking, "I need your help!" he panted from the exertion of running.

John did not mind the interruption at all, neither did the people he was talking to, "Who have we here?" John carefully took Anna from Simeon just as Lydia and Isaac arrived.

John cradled Anna in his arms, seeing instantly what was wrong and said, "In the name of Jesus, be healed!"

Isaac watched as Anna changed; the cut on her leg disappeared, the redness and swelling went, her face got its colour back and she looked peaceful! But she did not wake up! "Why isn't she awake?" blurted out Isaac, worried.

John looked at him and smiled, "You're her friend, aren't you?" Isaac nodded.

"Well, I think she will wake up when she's alone with you. She needs to be with someone she knows and can trust." John handed Anna gently back to Simeon and turned back to the people he had been talking to.

Simeon carried Anna home and laid her carefully down on the little straw mattress in the upstairs room where they all slept. He nodded at Isaac, took Lydia's hand, and led her out of the room.

Chapter Nine

Safe

For Anna, it seemed that no time had passed from the moment when Jesus had told her to trust him to the moment when she heard Isaac's whispered voice, "It's okay, you can wake up now."

She opened her eyes, and the first thing she saw was Isaac, her best friend, the one she knew she could trust above all others, except for Jesus of course. She remembered her dream with a pang of disappointment – she had not wanted the dream to end. Isaac watched her anxiously.

"Isaac? What's going on?" asked Anna, sitting up and noticing the room she was in for the first time. It was a big room with a small window, and she was sitting on a comfortable straw mattress!

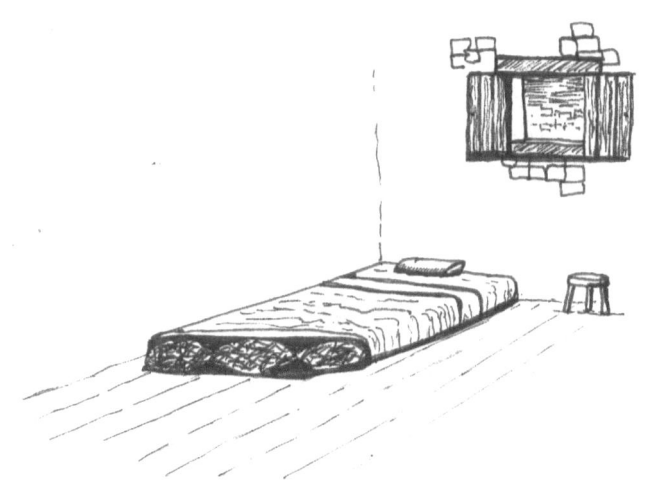

Isaac, who had been kneeling by the bed, got up off his knees and leapt around the room shouting, "Yes! It worked! Jesus really did heal you! Yes! Yes! Yes!" he yelled, punching the air.

Anna could not help but laugh at her friend, "What's going on?" she asked bewildered.

"I thought you were going to die, but Jesus made you better!"

"What? What happened? Where are we? This isn't our place You remembered, you found me! Did you find me? How did I get here?" Anna looked down at her leg, confused, "I cut my leg; I think... did I? Where's the cut? Did I dream it?"

"No, you didn't... and, yes, I did remember and Jesus healed you."

"I dreamt about Jesus."

"Did you?"

"It was lovely. So where are we?"

"Okay," said Isaac sitting on the end of the mattress, "what do you remember?"

"Well, there were these slave traders..." she automatically tensed, "are they here?"

"No, it's okay, you're completely safe."

"But they sold us to 'Angry Eyes!' I was so scared... you got away?"

"No, not really. But it's okay," he quickly said as he saw panic in Anna's eyes, "trust me, everything's fine."

Anna settled back down again, "I ran and ran, Isaac! I was so scared, I didn't know what to do, I couldn't even get any food, I was so hungry. Then I remembered our place and I went there but I kept falling asleep and then I felt so bad, and my leg hurt, and I was so hot, and then I don't remember any more...so where are we?"

"Okay, I'll tell you, but don't panic."

"What do you mean?"

Isaac took a deep breath, "You remember what happened on the special feast day before we were taken? You remember that apostle, one of Jesus' followers – Peter – he started talking to everyone explaining why Jesus died and that he had risen from the dead, and lots of people believed him and all over the place people were crying on their knees asking Jesus to forgive them?"

Anna nodded.

"Well, two of those people were Simeon and Lydia – or as we called them, - 'Mr and Mrs Angry Eyes'. Jesus has totally changed them! They're really nice now, in fact they came with me to find you, and Simeon carried you back to John who is one of Jesus' apostles, and he prayed for you, and you got better but didn't wake up. He told Simeon to take you home so you could wake up somewhere safe with just me so that you wouldn't be scared. So here we are, in Simeon and Lydia's house. Everything is alright, we are safe!" Isaac waited for the reaction from Anna. He stood up ready to catch her if she tried to run away again.

But she did not run. She did not say anything. After a while Isaac asked, "Anna, are you alright?"

Anna looked at him and said, "Jesus said I should trust him! Isaac, this time we could run away together."

"No Anna! Listen to me. You are safe! Everything is alright! We are totally safe now! Anna, I trust Jesus too now. Simeon and Lydia are good people, they love Jesus just like you do, and they are not angry anymore. They came with me to find you and rescue you, and Simeon carried you all the way home."

"But they bought us as slaves! What do you mean 'home'?"

"They bought us as slaves to rescue us so that no-one else could buy us, and this is their home, we are not their slaves!"

Anna began to cry, "Is it true? Are we really safe?"

"Yes, I promise you."

Isaac went to the top of the stairs, "Lydia? Could you come up please?" he called. He decided that it was better for Anna to meet them one at a time, and Lydia was smaller and less intimidating than Simeon.

Lydia walked into the room tentatively. She smiled at Anna, "Hello sweetheart, how are you feeling?"

"Alright," Anna replied in a small voice.

"I expect this is all a bit strange for you, isn't it?" Anna nodded, unsure of what to say.

"Well," Isaac said, "I'm going downstairs, I'll leave you to get to know one another. It's really okay, Anna," he reassured her.

"How's it going up there?" Simeon asked as Isaac came downstairs into the kitchen.

"Well, I think she believes me, that we're safe now. It took a bit of persuasion, she's still a bit scared. I thought I'd leave her with Lydia for a while. I think she's feeling a bit overwhelmed."

"Well done, lad!" said Simeon inviting him to come and sit with him.

Suddenly, Isaac felt exhausted and tearful. He roughly brushed away the tears that were starting to form, he did not want to cry again!

"Quite a day, eh?" said Simeon.

Isaac nodded, not trusting himself to speak. Simeon sat down next to him, "It's alright to cry, you know. I cried like a baby when I knew that Jesus had forgiven me!"

Try as he might, Isaac could not hold it in any longer, all the fear and uncertainty of the last couple of days when he thought he had lost Anna, came bubbling up, and he found himself once again, sobbing in the kitchen. Simeon pulled Isaac into a big hug and held him, letting him cry as much as he needed to.

Upstairs, Anna was listening to Lydia, "I understand that you're very unsure of me, Anna, and that's alright. But let me tell you what happened to me and Simeon a couple of days ago during the Feast, Isaac tells me you were both there…

Simeon and I have been married for quite a long time and have been unable to have any children of our own. To be honest, we had become very bitter and angry about that over the years and were very unhappy, but when we listened to Peter speaking about Jesus and telling us how much God loved us, it was as though a light went on in our hearts and we just knew that Peter was telling the truth. It's amazing how knowing you are loved can bring so much healing." Lydia paused to smile at Anna, then continued, "Just before all this happened, Simeon, without telling me, arranged to buy a slave because he needed extra help in the bakery. He had forgotten all about it until they turned up a couple of days ago. Since meeting Jesus, Simeon no longer wanted to own a slave, and when he told me, we knew that we wanted to rescue you and Isaac, so we decided to buy you to stop you being sold to anyone else. And now, here you are, safe and sound."

Anna did not know what to say, but she remembered her dream and how Jesus had been looking after her all the time. Was this part of his looking after her? She so wanted to believe it, so wanted a grown up to be in charge, so wanted to not have to beg for food to survive.

Suddenly her stomach rumbled and she realised how hungry she was. She put her hand on her belly.

"You must be hungry!" observed Lydia, "Would you like to come downstairs to have something to eat?"

Anna nodded, hoping Isaac was still downstairs, she felt braver when she was with him. She followed Lydia and found Isaac sitting talking to Simeon.

Anna looked around the room. It was much bigger than her house used to be, and there was more furniture than she had ever seen! Cabinets and shelves holding clay vases and copper pots of different sizes. There was a clay oven in the corner and Isaac and Simeon were sitting on stools around a table, not a low table like there had been at her house, but a large table about waist height to Lydia. Anna had never seen anything like it; it was so big, and they did not even have to sleep in this room!

Isaac turned and saw her, relieved that he had got all of his crying out of the way, "Hey Anna, how are you? Come and sit with me!" he patted the stool next to him.

Simeon introduced himself to Anna, "Hello Anna, I'm Simeon. Isaac's told me all about you, and I'm guessing Lydia's told you all about us?" Lydia nodded.

Anna froze where she was, scared of this large man. She looked at Simeon, directly into his eyes, she wanted to see if what Lydia had told her was true.

It was like looking at a different person! Anna had never forgotten Simeon's angry eyes; she had been terrified, but as she looked into his eyes now, she could see that all his anger had melted away. They were now warm, sparkling, happy eyes.

Anna realised that at this moment she had a choice to make. Was she going to trust these people? She looked at Isaac for reassurance and he smiled at her. Clearly, he had been won over by them.

"Hello," she said to Simeon in barely more than a whisper.

"Why don't you come and sit next to Isaac and we'll get you both something to eat," encouraged Simeon, pointing to the stool next to Isaac, as Anna had not moved since she had come into the room. Timidly, Anna crept towards Isaac and sat next to him as Simeon vacated his own stool to help Lydia prepare some food.

Soon, Isaac and Anna were talking together quietly like they always used to, catching up on their adventures.

Simeon and Lydia watched them, "I think she'll come round eventually," Lydia said to Simeon quietly as she prepared some food.

"I hope so, the poor child has been scared half to death."

"Can you believe what is actually happening to us?"

Simeon put his arm around Lydia, "Yes and no! Yes, because I know that Jesus has changed us, and no, because it just seems to have happened so quickly!"

The brand-new 'family' of four sat around the table together eating the flat bread and fruit. Isaac and Anna ate hungrily and very quickly.

"Slow down you two!" laughed Simeon, "The food's not going anywhere and there's a lot more where that came from!"

When the children had eaten their fill, Lydia spoke to them. "It's been a strange few days for you both...well for all of us actually," she said, "and I think it would be good to clean you up a bit and get you some new clothes."

Anna looked down at her tunic, you could no longer tell what colour it was meant to be, and it was torn in so many places. She put her hand on her hair and realised how tangled it was. She and Isaac had not bathed or washed their hair for an awfully long time. What would Mary have thought if she had known Anna had not brushed her hair for many weeks? Her father had never really cared about that kind of thing; it was Mary who had taught her about cleanliness.

Anna suddenly felt embarrassed; there was no way she was going to bathe properly in front of Isaac or Simeon! She must have shown it on her face, as Simeon said, "Come on Isaac, you and I will go and bathe in the baths, and Anna can clean up here."

Lydia warmed up a bowl of water and helped Anna out of her tunic. Lydia only just managed to stifle a gasp as she saw how pitifully thin Anna had become. It took them quite a while to get all the grime off!

"It's okay, Anna," she soothed, "we'll soon have you cleaned up. But I'm not sure what to do with your hair, it's so badly knotted I think we might have to cut some off."

Anna began to cry; she had been so brave up until now, but the thought of having to cut off her hair was just too much! She sobbed uncontrollably as Lydia held her in her arms.

Lydia said nothing, just held her, and eventually Anna calmed down.

"I'm sorry sweetheart, I'll do my best to take off as little as possible, but I will have to cut some off."

Anna nodded tearfully.

By the time Lydia had finished cutting her hair, Anna felt a lot better, especially when Lydia showed her what it looked like in a polished metal mirror.

"It will grow back quite quickly," reassured Lydia.

Anna nodded, "Thank you," she said shyly.

"Now, I have managed to borrow a tunic from our neighbours, I think it will be a bit big, but it will do for now and tomorrow you and I will go to the bazaar and get some new clothes sorted out for you and Isaac," said Lydia.

Anna loved the feel and the smell of a new tunic. She felt better than she had done for a long time – safe, clean and with a full stomach!

Just then, Simeon and Isaac came in. At least she thought it was Isaac, he looked quite different with shorter hair and a new tunic – and he was clean!

"Anna! Is that really you?" asked Isaac, amazed at how different she looked. Anna smiled shyly.

"You seemed to take a long time!" said Lydia with a smile, imagining that Simeon had probably bumped into some of their many new friends.

Simeon laughed, "Yes, we met a few of our friends on the way there and back!" Lydia smiled to herself. Friends were not something she and Simeon were used to.

"Well, I need to get to work," said Simeon, "I'm opening the bakery early tomorrow. Would you like to help me, Isaac? I'm sure Lydia and Anna have their own plans."

"Okay," said Isaac, intrigued.

Chapter Ten

Stories

Lydia and Anna spent the next couple of hours fetching water and preparing dinner. Lydia had said to Anna that she could just sit and watch if she was tired, but Anna wanted to help. It reminded her of being with Mary.

As they worked, Lydia chatted away, but Anna was still quite shy and a little unsure, so she only gave one-word answers. Anna knew that Jesus had told her to trust him, but she was struggling to trust Simeon and Lydia. There was a difference between trusting Jesus and trusting people!

Lydia understood Anna's reticence and was happy to give her the time she needed to adjust to her new circumstances.

That evening the four of them sat down to a delicious meal of beef and vegetable stew that Anna had helped Lydia prepare.

"This is really good," garbled Isaac through a mouthful of food. "Thank you," replied Lydia, struggling not to laugh at him!

Anna had never tasted anything so delicious! Even when she was with Mary who had been an excellent cook, they very rarely had meat and only a few vegetables – their diet had been mainly bread as it was the cheapest thing to make. She looked around the house again and realised that Simeon and Lydia must be very rich.

Isaac and Anna began yawning soon after dinner; they were tired after a long day, and they had never felt so full of food.

"Come on you two, time for bed. It's been quite a day!" said Lydia.

They hauled themselves up the stairs without argument as they were both so tired. Lydia had managed to acquire another straw mattress, so the children felt like they were living in luxury as they went to bed that night!

"Are we really safe here?" whispered Anna.

"Yes, don't worry, trust me," yawned Isaac. Within minutes, he was fast asleep, snoring gently. Anna did not think she would get to sleep quite so quickly but she followed just a few moments later from sheer exhaustion.

The next morning, both children woke at about the same time. They could hear noises downstairs so guessed that Lydia and Simeon were already up.

"It feels a bit strange waking up inside a house, doesn't it?" said Isaac.

"Yeah, it does, and also a house with more than one room and an upstairs!"

"I can't believe it's got three rooms if you include the bakery, and there's a barn next to it that belongs to them!"

"I think they've got quite a bit of money" said Anna in a whisper just in case Simeon or Lydia could hear.

"I know," replied Isaac, "can you believe what's happened to us?"

"No! It feels so strange. I keep expecting those slave traders to turn up though. What if they're still owed some money?" worried Anna.

"You've got more than just me looking after you now, you'll be okay."

Anna nodded, but still felt a little fearful and decided that she would not be going outside on her own for a while.

"What do we do now?" asked Anna.

"What do you mean?" replied Isaac.

"Well, can we just go downstairs into the kitchen?"

Isaac laughed, "Of course we can, silly! This is our home now, Simeon and Lydia said so!"

"Are you sure they're okay Isaac? You remember what Simeon was like?"

"Anna, he's not the same man now. You saw how nice he is, and he searched with me for two days trying to find you, and he wouldn't give up. Then he carried you to John and then home here. You don't need to be scared of him. Trust me, we're safe now."

And with that, Isaac climbed off his mattress and walked towards the doorway. Anna followed and they went downstairs to find some freshly baked bread waiting for them. Their eyes widened in delight. Anna's worry was temporarily forgotten, as they tucked into the bread. It felt strange not to feel hungry all the time!

After breakfast, they chatted with Lydia about the day ahead.

"Well, I would like to go shopping and buy some material to make you two some clothes. Would you like to come with me?" asked Lydia.

Anna was torn, she was so excited about going shopping for some material, but she was also scared of bumping into the slave traders. She hesitated before she replied. Lydia noticed the conflict in her eyes, "What is it, Anna? Don't you want to come?"

"I do, I really do, It's just…."

"She's scared she'll meet the slave traders," Isaac finished the sentence for her.

"Sweetheart, you don't need to worry about them, I will look after you." said Lydia getting down on one knee in front of Anna and putting her hands on her shoulders so that she could look her directly in the eyes, "I'll tell you what, why don't you hold my hand so that you feel safe?",

Anna nodded and smiled, "Okay." she agreed. She looked expectantly at Isaac, excitement in her eyes but did not see the same reflected back, "Are you coming?"

"Er ..."

Lydia laughed, "You don't have to come, Isaac, you could go and help Simeon instead!"

"Thank goodness for that!" said Isaac with relief as he went into the bakery.

Anna held on tightly to Lydia's hand as they went to visit the bazaar. She was struggling to believe that she was no longer in danger.

Very soon though, all fear was forgotten as Lydia helped her choose some material for her new clothes. Anna had never owned anything made from such beautiful material. So many different colours and beautiful silky textures! She knew that she would feel like a princess wearing clothes made from this material!

Lydia was thoroughly enjoying herself, having a child to spoil, something she had longed for, for many years. She looked down at Anna touching the material, her eyes wide in excitement.

"I wonder if her own mother ever took her shopping?" she thought. She realised that she did not know Anna's story, only that she was now an orphan with no family.

After well over an hour of shopping, having chosen some material for Anna, Lydia remembered that Isaac would need something quite different! After finding material suitable for him, Lydia and Anna headed back home.

Anna had enjoyed her trip out enormously and she was almost reluctant to go back but she could not wait to see Isaac and show him the materials that would be used to make clothes for them both.

As they drew near to the bakery, they heard laughter. For a moment Lydia wondered who it could be, it was so long since she had heard Simeon laugh like that, a real belly laugh. Then as she listened more closely, she could also hear a higher pitched laugh of a young boy.

She and Anna looked at one another, puzzled. As they went into the bakery, they saw Isaac and Simeon, picking up flour with their hands from the broken sack on the floor and throwing it at one another. They were both covered from head to toe!

Lydia could not believe her eyes! Her husband, wasting perfectly good flour! In the past, if that kind of thing had happened, he would be raging and bemoaning the waste!

"Jesus, you really have changed him!" she marvelled to herself.

Simeon and Isaac stopped when they saw Lydia and Anna. Isaac went to throw some flour at Anna, a huge grin on his face.

"Don't you dare!" said Anna laughing, "We've got brand new material here that we're going to make into gorgeous clothes and you're not going to spoil it with your flour!"

"I guess we'd better clear this up lad, before we get into any more trouble! Or get any more customers!" Simeon grinned at Isaac.

Isaac reluctantly agreed, still amazed at Simeon's reaction to his dropping and splitting the sack of flour. He had instinctively cowered away from Simeon in the corner and had been astounded when Simeon, after pausing for a moment, had picked up a handful of the flour and thrown it at him with a huge laugh.

When they had finished cleaning up, Isaac asked Simeon the question uppermost in his mind, "Why didn't you get angry with me when I dropped the flour sack?"

Simeon looked at him thoughtfully and confessed, "Well to be honest, I was about to get angry, and then something, or perhaps I should say, someone, stopped me. Jesus showed me that it was an accident, you didn't do it on purpose, and it didn't really matter! It's just a bit of flour! In the past, I would have been livid at the waste, but now, well, things like love and forgiveness are much more important to me! All my priorities seem to have changed. I used to get angry all the time, but

Jesus has done something in my heart, I can't explain, it's hard to put into words…."

Isaac smiled; he could see that Simeon had changed. They did not get the opportunity to talk any longer, as more customers arrived who looked quizzically at their floury appearance!

It had been an exceptionally busy day and Simeon closed the bakery early having sold all of the bread that they had made by mid-afternoon.

"What about you, Isaac, what's your story?" asked Simeon, as he closed the serving hatch where customers came to buy the bread.

"Well, I lived with my mum and my grandparents…" began Isaac.

"Wait, hold that thought, I think Lydia would like to hear your story as well if that's okay?"

"Yes, of course," said Isaac; he had no problem telling Lydia too.

"Come on then, let's go in and find the ladies."

Lydia and Anna had spread the material out on the large table in the kitchen, and Lydia was skilfully marking out the shapes for the new tunics. Anna was hopping from one foot to the other, barely able to contain her excitement! She could not stop touching the material, and Lydia was laughing at her delight.

Lydia looked round as Simeon and Isaac entered the kitchen, "Are you finished for the day?" she enquired in surprise.

"Yes, we sold everything, there is not a single piece of bread left!" said Isaac proudly.

Simeon chuckled, "I think I'll have to make extra tomorrow, we had a few disappointed late-comers today as there was nothing left for them."

Anna stopped hopping around and looked up, "Look at all this material Isaac! I'm going to help Lydia make some clothes with it! I can sew a little bit, Mary taught me."

"Yes, you are," smiled Lydia, "but for now we need to put this material away, we don't want to get it dirty when we get dinner ready later."

Lydia sent Simeon and Isaac to clean off the flour that was still covering them, while she and Anna put the material away. A short while later, they all sat down at the table together to have a drink, as Lydia had a little time before she needed to prepare dinner.

"Isaac was just about to tell me his story," said Simeon, "I thought it would be good for you to hear it too, Lydia, I guess you already have, Anna?"

Anna nodded but was happy to hear Isaac's story again.

"Well, I lived with my mum and my grandparents," Isaac began for the second time, "My dad died when I was young, I don't really remember him. Then my grandparents died because they got old, then my mum got leprosy, so she had to go and live outside the city in the caves with the other lepers, then I went to live with some neighbours, and they wouldn't let me visit her in case I caught leprosy." Isaac took a deep breath, his lip quivered a little, but he pulled himself together and carried on, "One day, they said that my mum had died, and they threw me out, so I had to live on the streets. I just kept begging for food or money and sometimes stealing," he glanced at Simeon who chuckled, "...and finding places to sleep. I just tried to stay out of the way of the slave traders that my neighbours had threatened to sell me to. Then I met Anna and we stuck together because she was hiding from slave traders, too."

"You must have been so scared and hungry!" said Lydia.

"Well, we got used to it really, and we got pretty good at persuading people to give us money."

"Well, YOU did" interrupted Anna.

Isaac laughed, "Yeah, you weren't so good at it! Anyway, we just spent our days trying to survive and searching for Jesus, because Anna was convinced that he could help us."

"Did you get to see Jesus?" asked Simeon.

"Yes, we did!" said Anna, "We saw him when he came to Jerusalem riding on that donkey and the people were cheering and putting palm branches down; oh, it was amazing! And, he looked straight at me, I think he recognised me from the first time I saw him."

"You've seen him more than once?" asked Lydia.

"Actually, three times. The first time I saw him, I was with my dad. The second time was when he came into Jerusalem, and the third time was when he was crucified," Anna's voice broke, "he did nothing wrong; he was so kind, and he helped people, but they still crucified him and there was nothing Isaac and I could do to stop it! The worst bit was, we knew the chief priests were after him, we heard them talking about it. We tried to warn Jesus, but we couldn't find him! We even told someone, but they just laughed and said Jesus could take care of himself. But he still died, and we couldn't stop it. I don't know why God let that happen."

"You're right, Anna, God could have stopped it happening, and I believe Jesus could have called down a whole host of angels to rescue him, but he didn't. Peter told us that he chose to die for all of us," Simeon swept his arm round the table, "that's how much he loves us." Anna just nodded a little tearfully.

Isaac continued with his story, "After Jesus died, we didn't really know what to do. It was hard, especially for Anna. When we heard rumours about Jesus coming alive again, Anna was happier because she believed the rumours were true. I wasn't sure myself until the day of the feast, and then as I listened to Peter, I just knew that Jesus was alive. Of course, I didn't have much time to think about it because that's when the slave traders found us and chased us and caught us. They shackled and gagged us and threw us into a cellar where we were kept until they brought us to you." Isaac was inadvertently rubbing his wrists where the shackles had been.

Simeon grimaced, and Lydia had tears in her eyes, as they listened to Isaac, "You must have been so frightened!" Lydia said.

"We were!" said Anna, "It was horrible!" she shuddered. They sat silently for a while as Lydia, who was sitting next to Anna, put her arm around her.

So, what's your story, Anna?" asked Simeon, interrupting the silence, "How did you come to meet Isaac? What happened to you?"

Anna breathed in deeply and took a moment to compose her thoughts, "I lived with my dad. I never knew my mum because she died when I was born. We lived next door to Mary, and she looked after me and taught me how to bake bread and clean the house. We were okay, dad earnt a bit of money, he was a really good carpenter until he injured his hand, then he had trouble getting work and I think he started to drink too much..." Anna stopped, suddenly embarrassed; she wasn't sure she should have told them that part of her story, but after a reassuring squeeze from Lydia, she continued, "One day I was coming home from fetching water and Mary pulled me into her house and hid me behind a blanket. She told me there were two men looking for me because my dad owed them money. My dad had been killed that morning by some Roman soldiers. The men realised they were never going to get their money back from my dad, so they decided that they would take me instead and sell me as a slave."

"Mary pretended that she didn't know me, and when the men left, she arranged for a friend of hers to smuggle me out of the village and bring me to Jerusalem. He was hoping some people he knew could take me in, but while he was looking for them, I ran away because I was worried they might not want me or would sell me to the slave traders. Mary had told me not to come back to my village, she said it wasn't safe anymore. I was so scared, but things got a lot better when I met Isaac." Anna looked at Simeon fearfully, there was a question she wanted to ask but was afraid to.

Before she had a chance to ask him, Simeon guessed what the question was and reassured her, "Anna, I paid those men every penny that your dad owed, and more. You don't have to worry. They will not come to take you away. You are totally safe now here with us."

Anna could not fully take in what Simeon had just said to her. Was she really free? Was she really safe? Why had Simeon done this for her?

"You two are not our slaves, just because we bought you. We want to give you both a home here with us - if you would like that" Simeon added.

Isaac responded first, "Yes, I'd really like that," he said with a huge grin.

Anna did not know what to say, she so desperately wanted to believe that she was safe here with Simeon and Lydia, but she was still scared and struggling to trust them, especially Simeon. She couldn't erase the memory of his 'angry eyes' when she and Isaac had stolen his bread. After all, she had trusted her father before he began to drink; and look how that turned out!

Simeon could see the struggle she was going through, and he understood, "Anna, it's okay, it takes time to trust someone."

Anna just nodded, she felt she was being unfair to this couple who had rescued her, but she could not help how she was feeling.

"Right then, it's time to start getting dinner ready." said Lydia sensing Anna's turmoil and realising that she would need some time to begin to fully trust them.

Anna felt relieved at the change of subject and was grateful to Lydia for moving on. The four of them worked together and were very soon sitting down to another delicious meal.

Chapter Eleven

A New Life

That evening, shortly after they had finished their meal, two of their new friends, Andrew and Naomi, called in to invite Simeon and Lydia to come with them to a friend's house to meet some other new believers.

"Andrew, Naomi, I'd like you to meet Isaac and Anna," said Simeon, briefly explaining how they had come to live with them.

"Good to meet you both!" said Andrew ruffling their hair, "You can all come then!"

The six of them set off together, they did not have far to walk. Anna felt nervous about meeting other people, but Isaac was excited.

"Do you think it will be okay?" Anna asked Isaac quietly as they walked next to one another.

"Why wouldn't it be? We're quite safe, we're with Simeon and Lydia, they're not going to let anything bad happen to us." Isaac looked at Anna appraisingly, "You still don't trust them, do you?"

"I really want to Isaac, I do, and I think I trust Lydia, sort of. But I still find Simeon a bit scary! You remember what he was like!"

"Yes, but Simeon's not like that now! In that dream you had, didn't Jesus tell you to trust him?"

"He did, and I do, but I don't trust anyone else except you, and maybe Lydia, a bit."

"Then will you trust me when I tell you that we can trust Simeon as well?"

Anna thought about what Isaac said but then she just shrugged, unconvinced. Anyway, she did not want to talk about it anymore and felt a little cross that Isaac had trusted Simeon so easily.

They walked on in silence until they approached a house. It was smaller than Simeon and Lydia's home, and only appeared to have one large room that was crammed full of people. Some were standing, some were sitting on the floor, some were even perched on the large window-sills, and others were just leaning in the doorway. There did not appear to be any more space, but somehow, people made room for the six of them, and they squeezed in. Anna had to sit on Lydia's lap, and despite the number of people, everyone was quietly listening to a man speaking...

"...so, when I heard Peter talking, I just knew that what he was saying was true. It was like I could hide nothing from Jesus, and I could see all the things I'd done ..." the man hesitated and his voice broke as he continued, "I think a lot of you know how, when I collected the taxes from you, I took more than I should, basically I was stealing! And there I was, standing before Jesus asking him to forgive me, I could see how bad I was, but Jesus still forgave me! I feel like a totally different person now, I can't explain it! But I'm so grateful to Jesus and I'll pay back the money I stole. I'll give back what I took from you, I'm so sorry..."

Those near the man hugged him, laughing and crying with him. They heard more stories from others all repeating similar experiences, all with gratitude to Jesus for rescuing them. At some point people started to sing in worship to God.

Anna had forgotten her worries, and joined in worshipping Jesus, not knowing the words to the songs, although, to be fair, it seemed that a lot of people were just singing their own songs in their own words! Anna closed her eyes and felt as though Jesus was standing right there in the room with them all. She did not want to leave, no-one did.

They were enjoying the peace that had settled on the room, when suddenly they were disturbed by a young boy bursting through the doorway, out of breath, "Chief priest's men!" he panted, "on their way!"

Quickly and quietly, with only brief goodbyes, everyone dispersed to their own homes. Anna had been puzzled when Simeon picked her up and whisked her away out of the house as Lydia and Isaac had followed after them.

She was even more puzzled and alarmed when they arrived at their house and Simeon ushered them inside and told them all to be quiet. He put Anna down, quickly bolted the door and stood with his ear against it. Isaac, Anna, and Lydia stood still in the darkness hardly daring to breathe! It was not until Simeon turned away from the door, lit a lamp, and gazed at Anna with a look of concern, that she realised she was visibly shaking.

"Anna, you're safe, everything's okay," said Simeon as he put his hands on her shoulders and stooped down to look her in the eyes to reassure her.

Anna began to calm down.

"What happened?" asked Isaac, "Why did we have to leave? Why are we running from the chief priests' men? What's going on?"

"There's no need to panic!" reassured Simeon, "We were just being careful."

But Isaac noticed the quick glance he gave Lydia that indicated he may not be telling them the whole story.

"The religious leaders don't particularly like us meeting together with other believers." said Lydia trying to make light of the situation for the sake of Anna.

Isaac thought that the sudden ending of the gathering and the sense of fear of the chief priests' men, meant that things were more serious than Simeon and Lydia were letting on. Anna appeared to accept Lydia's explanation and seemed to relax, so Isaac decided to keep his concerns to himself for now.

Anna yawned, suddenly feeling very tired. "Right, bedtime, you two!" said Simeon.

"I'm not tired!" protested Isaac, but with a look from Simeon, he reluctantly followed Anna up the stairs and climbed onto his comfy mattress. Anna was asleep within moments but sleep eluded Isaac. He could hear the low voices of Simeon and Lydia talking in the kitchen, so he decided to creep downstairs to see if he could hear anything. He knew that they were hiding something from him and Anna!

Isaac sat on the stairs, getting as close as he could without being seen, and listened hard.

"I just don't want to worry them; they've been through enough! Especially Anna, she's like a frightened little mouse!" said Lydia.

"I know, and she still doesn't trust me, sometimes she looks at me with such fear!" replied Simeon.

"I know love, but give her time, I'm sure it will get better."

They were silent for a while, and Isaac worried that they might be about to come upstairs. But then they returned to their conversation....

"We should tell them something about the situation though, just so that they're careful. Even if we just tell Isaac. I mean, Anna's not going to go anywhere without him, is she?" said Lydia.

"I'm not sure. Is Isaac old enough to know the whole story?" asked Simeon.

"Yes! I am old enough!" burst out Isaac before he could stop himself. He clamped his hand over his mouth, but it was too late. Simeon came to the bottom of the stairs, a mixture of annoyance and amusement on his face. He beckoned to Isaac who came sheepishly down the stairs and into the kitchen.

"Sit," said Simeon pointing to a stool, "Isaac, I told you to go to bed. It's not good to listen to private conversations!" he paused as if considering what to do, "However, I know you're curious, and I'll let it go this time."

"I'm sorry, I just saw the look you gave Lydia before and I knew you weren't telling us everything and I didn't want to say anything in front of Anna because she's scared enough and she's only a child, but I'm a man now, and I can take anything you have to tell me." said Isaac defensively.

Simeon looked at him appraisingly for a few seconds and put a hand on his shoulder. He smiled and said, "Yes okay, you are practically a man!" he took a breath and continued, "The chief priests and the Romans don't like what's going on with the followers of Jesus. They were hoping that as they had got rid of Jesus, his followers would give up on him, so you can imagine how angry they are that more and more people are believing in Jesus every day. They are trying to stop us gathering together, which is why we must do it in secret. It's okay, we just need to be a bit careful, that's all."

"But what about Jesus' apostles? What about Peter and John? They've been standing up talking to crowds of people in the middle of the day and in the temple! They're not doing things in secret, if they carry on, they could get arrested!" said Isaac.

"Yes, they could. In fact, it's probably only a matter of time. The chief priests are probably looking for an opportunity like they did with Jesus." responded Simeon.

"So, what do we do?" asked Isaac, "Do we stop seeing other believers?"

"Goodness me no!" said Lydia, "We don't have to be scared, just wise, that's all."

"We will follow the Holy Spirit and trust him with our lives." added Simeon.

"But we don't tell Anna all this." said Isaac.

"No, I think it's best to keep it between us." said Lydia.

Isaac noticed that Simeon and Lydia often mentioned the Holy Spirit, he longed to talk to them about him, but he knew the conversation was coming to an end and he was about to be told to go back up to bed. Although he had only known Simeon for a few days, one thing he was sure about, was that he was not going to be allowed to avoid bed for the second time that night!

"Up you go then!" said Simeon predictably.

Isaac reluctantly complied, a little disappointed, a little scared, a little excited at everything he had just heard. He wondered if his life would ever become boring.

Anna slept until late the next morning; when she awoke the sun was streaming in through the window. It took her a while to realise where she was.

She looked around for Isaac, but he was not there. She got out of bed and went downstairs. Lydia was there alone looking at the material they had bought the day before, "Morning, sweetheart," she smiled at Anna.

"Morning," yawned Anna, "where's Isaac?"

"With Simeon, they've been up for a while, sleepyhead! They're baking bread and selling it to the customers. Would you like some breakfast?"

"Yes please."

Anna sat herself down at the table and Lydia gave her some delicious fresh bread and a cup of goat's milk.

"This is the best bread I've ever tasted!" said Anna as she gobbled it down quickly.

"Anna! Slow down, you don't have to rush your food! I will give you three meals a day, there is plenty of food here, and no-one is going to take it from you!"

Anna stopped mid chew, "Sorry!" Lydia smiled at her.

"Are we making the clothes today?" Anna asked her.

"We'll make a start with the tunics now, then I wondered if you'd like to help in the bakery this afternoon?"

"I'd like that, I used to help Mary bake bread all the time, I haven't done that for ages."

"Lovely, well now you've finished breakfast, let's clean the table and start sewing."

It did not take long for the two of them to make a couple of tunics each for Isaac and Anna. Anna was delighted with her new clothes that fit her perfectly. She had never owned more than one tunic at a time, now she had two with a promise of two more! Anna put them upstairs carefully on her mattress and came back down, eager to help in the bakery. They went next door to find Simeon baking and Isaac serving customers.

"He's a natural with people, that boy is, not so much with baking though!" laughed Simeon.

"Well, you've got two extra pairs of hands now," said Lydia.

Anna definitely preferred baking bread to serving customers. Simeon was impressed with her baking skills, although she could not knead the dough as well as Simeon with his strong arms. She tried to help Isaac serve customers but was incredibly shy and got flustered with handling all that money! Not all girls had the opportunity to have an education. Only boys were allowed to go to the synagogue to learn to read and write; girls had to be taught at home, and Anna had only been taught how to cook, clean, and sew.

The bakery did not close at lunchtime as that was when it was at its busiest. Isaac soon found out that Simeon had a particularly good reputation as a baker, and people would go out of their way to come and find his bakery as the bread was of such good quality. There was no sitting down to a meal at lunchtime, they grabbed food when they could and worked for the rest of the day.

Isaac could not believe the amount of money they were getting; he had never seen so much! No wonder they lived in a two-storey house!

Everyone was tired at the end of the day, and relieved to be sitting around the old wooden table enjoying some lamb and vegetables expertly cooked by Lydia.

"Well, that was busier than usual!" laughed Simeon, "There seems to be more customers every week! I think I might need to get some extra help; I don't want you children wearing yourselves out!"

Both children protested saying they had enjoyed the work and they were not at all tired - which would have been more believable had they not both yawned as they said it!

"Simeon, I noticed a couple of children in the street outside the bakery today. They didn't come to buy any bread, and I think they were begging for food from our customers. I'm wondering if they're homeless like we were. If I see them again, is it okay if I give them some bread?" asked Isaac through a mouthful of lamb.

"Yes of course, but also, see what you can find out about them. We may be able to help in other ways."

Lydia looked up from her plate of food, "You know, there could be lots of people we could help. What about that poor old lady down the street? You know, the one who lost her husband recently, she looks starving, we could take her some food."

"I could take some now if you like," suggested Isaac eagerly.

Simeon laughed, "I love your enthusiasm Isaac, but if you knock on her door at this time of night, you'll scare her half to death!"

"Maybe Anna and I could visit her some time, would you like that, Anna?" asked Lydia. Anna nodded.

"You're a bit quiet," observed Isaac, talking to Anna, "What's the matter?"

"Nothing."

"Come on, what is it?" he pushed.

"I liked working in the bakery, but please can I just stick to baking bread?" Anna directed her question at Simeon.

"Of course, you're an excellent baker anyway, so you're best helping me with the bread. I don't suppose you had the chance to learn numbers or reading or writing, did you?" asked Simeon, sensing Anna's embarrassment.

"Mary didn't know how to read and write, but she did teach me about money. But my dad was too busy to teach me anything!" explained Anna defensively.

"I could teach you, if you like?" suggested Lydia.

"Yes please!" Anna's eyes lit up; it was something she thought she would never be able to do. She had always found it a little unfair that the boys in her village got to go to the small synagogue to be taught, and the girls had to stay at home to learn to bake and keep house. Anna had always wanted to learn all the things that the boys were able to learn.

"We've got a little surprise for you two when you go up to bed tonight," said Simeon. Isaac and Anna looked at one another, what on earth could he mean?

Simeon and Lydia just grinned at the children, "You've had a long day, we'll clear up the kitchen, why don't you go straight up to bed?"

For the first time, Isaac and Anna did not need telling twice. They raced up the stairs and burst into the room.

"What?!" yelled Isaac and Anna at the same time as they saw that their straw mattresses had been replaced by two brand new wooden beds! They could not believe what they were seeing. Only rich people had such luxuries! They were speechless as they felt the wool stuffed mattresses on the beds and the soft woollen blankets and pillows. Surely, only kings and queens lived like this didn't they?

Both children laughed in delight at such extravagance!

"Do you remember sleeping on the hard floor behind those old baskets?" said Isaac.

"And in that old stable with no roof? And getting cold, even with your cloak?" laughed Anna, "Can you believe this?"

They turned round to see Simeon and Lydia standing in the doorway smiling at their delight. "Thank you!" said Isaac, "this is amazing, we've never ever slept in beds!"

"And these woollen blankets are so soft! And such soft pillows!" laughed Anna.

"When did you do this? We didn't notice anything," asked Isaac.

"You were busy in the bakery when these arrived!" said Lydia.

"We're glad you like your new beds, now, get in them, and try and get some sleep!" said Simeon, chuckling.

That night the children had the best night's sleep they had ever had.

Chapter Twelve

The Barn

Over the next few days, the new family of four settled into a happy routine.

Isaac would help Simeon in the bakery, and Anna would help Lydia feed and milk the goats, and with the sewing and cooking. If there was time, she would also help in the bakery.

They were becoming used to being part of a wider family of believers. They would often be in each other's houses, eating and praying together, sharing bread and wine with one another.

"What does it mean when we share the bread and wine with each other?" Isaac asked one day as the family of four sat down together.

"Well, as Peter explained it to us; at the last Passover meal he had with Jesus, he said that Jesus took a piece of bread and held it up and broke it into pieces and gave a piece to each of them, and as he did so, he told them it was like his body that was going to be broken for them. Then he took a cup of wine and said that the wine was like his blood that was about to be poured out for them. He told them that whenever they had bread and wine together, they should remember that he died for them."

"Did Jesus think they would forget what he did? And why would they want to remember him dying?" asked Anna.

Simeon replied, "Those are really good questions. No, I don't think Jesus thought they would forget what he did, but maybe over time we might forget why he did it. Remember, he died so that we could be forgiven for all the things we've done wrong. By dying, Jesus opened the way for us to get to know God, I remember Peter saying we could now come home to our heavenly Father...."

"So," interrupted Isaac, "It's a bit like Anna and I going through all that horrible stuff, but Jesus worked it all out so that we could come home to you and Lydia? Because if we hadn't been caught by the slave traders we wouldn't be here, and if Jesus hadn't gone through dying on the cross, we wouldn't be forgiven and have a way back to God who's our Father!"

"That's a really good way of putting it, Isaac!" said Simeon, "Except coming home to your heavenly Father is a lot better than coming home to us!"

"So, we didn't need to worry about not being able to tell Jesus that the chief priests were after him, because he knew he was going to die the night before it happened!" said Anna, feeling a little relieved.

"Apparently, he knew long before that night that he was going to die for us!" said Simeon.

"So, when he came to Jerusalem and everyone was cheering and welcoming him, he knew they were going to turn on him and kill him?" asked Anna with tears in her eyes.

"Yes," said Lydia quietly as she put her arms around Anna.

Everyone sat quietly for a while, thinking about what Jesus had done for them.

Isaac broke the silence by asking another question, "So why do we all share one piece of bread and why do we all drink from the same cup of wine?"

"Well, I think it's because we're one big family. Jesus is the head of the family, and we're all members of it, so we share the bread and wine together." said Simeon.

Isaac laughed, "Imagine how big the loaf of bread would have to be if we shared it with all the believers in Jerusalem at the same time!"

Simeon chuckled, "Even I couldn't bake a loaf that big!"

"What else did Jesus tell his apostles to do?" asked Anna.

"Goodness me!" said Lydia, "I think Jesus told them so many things."

"One of the things he did say, was to baptise people when they believed in Jesus. Lydia and I were baptised, but we haven't baptised you two yet, I think that would be a good thing to do." said Simeon.

"That would be great!" replied Isaac.

"When could we do that?" asked Anna.

"Leave it with me, I'll try and arrange something for tonight, it would be good to get some of our friends involved as well," said Simeon.

That evening, after dark, Isaac and Anna were baptised in a pool along with some other new believers. They had found a quiet place out of the way of the religious authorities so they would not be disturbed. The children had found it incredibly exciting even though Anna had been scared of going under the water. There were fourteen people in all being baptised.

As Isaac and Anna came up out of the water, they were also baptised in the Holy Spirit, just like Simeon, Lydia, and hundreds of others had experienced on the day of the Feast.

"Wow," said Isaac, "I can't stop shaking! Was that what it was like for you?" he asked Lydia as they walked home from the pool.

"No, it was more like this huge weight on me, not crushing me, but holding me to the ground, I couldn't have moved if I'd wanted to. And I didn't want to. I remember all this joy bubbling up inside me and I couldn't help myself singing, shouting, praising God at the top of my voice, and speaking in these strange languages that I had never learnt. One minute I was laughing, then I was crying, then I was laying in the dirt face down in awe of God, and in that moment, I knew without a doubt that he loved me and that my life had changed forever. I will never forget that day!" laughed Lydia.

"I feel like all this power is going through me!" said Isaac, "It's like a fire, and somehow, it makes me feel really brave, and makes me want to go and tell everyone about Jesus."

"That sounds wonderful Isaac," said Simeon as he caught up with the two of them. He was carrying Anna who had fallen asleep as it was getting quite late. None of them had had the chance to talk to Anna to find out what her experience had been, they had watched as she had seemed to be totally overwhelmed by the Holy Spirit and had lain on the ground completely still for about an hour.

As they approached the bakery, their friend Andrew was waiting for them. "Andrew, what are you doing here this late?" asked Simeon in a hushed voice.

"It's best we talk inside," whispered Andrew.

They went inside the house quietly and Andrew closed the door, looking around as if checking that they were not followed.

"What is it, Andrew?" asked Lydia as Simeon took Anna upstairs and laid her on her bed. Isaac was relieved that he was not sent to bed.

"I'll just wait for Simeon…. ah here he is…well, Peter and John were arrested earlier. They healed a crippled beggar at the temple gate, and of course crowds gathered, and they started to tell people about Jesus. But then the chief priests came, they were so angry with Peter and John, so they had them arrested and took them away! But it didn't stop hundreds more people believing in Jesus!"

Isaac gasped, "So what are they going to do with them?"

"We don't know."

Andrew spent the rest of the night with Simeon and Lydia, none of them getting any sleep. Isaac was carried up to bed at some point when he fell asleep at the table they were sitting around. The adults continued to talk and pray until morning, concerned for Peter and John, yet also delighted that so many more people had believed in Jesus.

Andrew went back to his house the next morning and a very tired Simeon and Lydia started the baking. Isaac woke up late. The only one who was wide awake and totally oblivious to the previous night's events was Anna, who skipped downstairs as bright as a button.

"You all look so tired," she observed, "I don't remember getting home last night, did you have to carry me home Simeon? Did you all have to take it in turns to carry me? Is that why you're so tired?"

Simeon laughed, "A little thing like you? You think I can't carry you all the way home? It's like carrying a couple of sparrows!"

"Is there anymore news?" asked Isaac.

"What are you talking about?" asked Anna.

"Isaac…." said Lydia, giving him a warning look, "we'll talk later."

"News? Talk about what later? What is it? What aren't you telling me?" asked Anna sharply.

"Sorry!" said Isaac, "I wasn't thinking, I'm so tired."

"What do you mean? Please will someone just tell me what's going on?" demanded Anna.

"Okay, we didn't want you to be worried that's all. Last night Peter and John got arrested for healing a crippled beggar and telling people about Jesus. They were thrown in jail, and we don't know what's going to happen to them," said Simeon.

"Oh…" Anna's face fell, but then she surprised everyone by saying, "well, we worried when Jesus got arrested, but he trusted God and although he was crucified, he was raised from the dead and that was all God's plan for him so I guess we shouldn't worry about Peter and John because I expect God has a plan for them too."

Everyone around the table was stunned. Simeon shook his head and marvelled at the child- like faith of Anna, "You are absolutely right young lady! Let us get on with our day and leave Peter and John in God's hands!"

It was halfway through the morning when they got news of Peter and John. Andrew came by with a huge grin on his face. He laughed as he told them, "It was amazing! Apparently, during the night, an angel came and let Peter and John out of jail. So, this morning, they went back to the temple courts to carry on telling people about Jesus. The chief priests knew nothing about this, so when they sent the temple guards to go and get Peter and John out of jail, they weren't there! The door was locked, the jailor said no-one had been in or out, but they weren't there, and then someone told them they'd seen Peter and John in the temple courts. So, they re-arrested them and warned them not to tell anyone else about Jesus and then let them go!"

"An angel!" exclaimed the children together, "Wow!"

"They're not going to stop telling people about Jesus though, are they?" asked Anna.

"No, of course not!" said Lydia, "It would take a lot more than the threat of jail to do that!"

"That's brilliant!" said Simeon.

That evening, Anna spoke up at the dinner table, "I meant to say something first thing this morning," she said, "but we got a bit caught up with this whole Peter and John thing. Last night, something happened to me."

"Oh, yes of course. I told Simeon and Lydia what happened to me, but you were asleep!" said Isaac.

"I was, and I'd had the most wonderful time!"

"We saw you lying on the ground for ages, you seemed perfectly happy, so we left you alone," said Lydia.

"I'm glad you did. It felt like I was being filled up with God's love right to the tips of my fingers and my toes, and he told me something. It wasn't like I could hear his voice, I just knew in here," she patted her chest, "that it was him talking to me," she suddenly became a little shy and looked at Simeon who instinctively reached out his hand and held hers.

Anna smiled, "I know I can trust you now," she said simply, "I was afraid, but I'm not now. Somehow, the Holy Spirit makes me feel braver and I know you're not like my dad or like those slave traders, and I believe you when you say you will keep me safe."

"Anna, thank you for saying that, it means the world to me. I will do my absolute best for you, I'm sure I will make mistakes, but I will never intentionally hurt you," said Simeon with a break in his voice. Lydia made no attempt to stop the tears flowing down her cheeks.

Every day more and more people believed in Jesus. Simeon and Lydia made many new friends and were always having people round for meals and going to other believer's houses. They spent a lot of time praying and worshipping together, never in the same place twice in a row, constantly moving around, keeping out of the way of the authorities.

Simeon and Lydia were hearing stories of many believers selling property or land that they owned and giving the money to the apostles to distribute among the poor. There were so many people who struggled to afford to eat, but those that had plenty shared what they had so no-one went without.

Simeon and Lydia owned three additional properties that they rented out to other people and had decided to sell them and give the money to the apostles so it could be shared amongst the believers who had truly little or nothing at all. They had taken all their money back from their bankers and given that away too. It had not been without a struggle! For his entire adult life, Simeon had focused mainly on two things – to become the best baker in the city and to get rich. He had achieved both but realised that neither had given him the satisfaction or contentment that he desired. There were always more people to impress with his baking and there was always more money to make and invest. It took a little while for Simeon to get to the place where he could trust God to provide everything he needed.

Lydia laughed as Simeon had given the last of their money to the apostles, "Can you believe what you've just done?!"

"I know, all the years I've worked hard and saved and held on to my inheritance and here I am, happy to give it away, having to trust Jesus to keep providing for us!" Simeon chuckled.

"I love it!" said Lydia, "I've never been so happy!"

"Should we sell the barn too?" asked Lydia a few days later as she was helping Simeon in the bakery.

"I'm not sure, I knew for certain that we should sell the other three houses but for some reason I'm not sure about the barn."

"I'm not sure either," said Lydia.

Just before the bakery closed, Simeon had a new customer that he recognised as John, the apostle who had healed Anna.

"I recognise you!" John said, "I've seen you before, you brought your little girl to me when she was sick. I'm John."

"I know who you are! I'm Simeon," he laughed, waving away the money John was trying to give him for the bread he was buying. "You don't need to pay, it's a gift."

"Thank you, Simeon!" replied John, "So how is your daughter?"

"She's not exactly my daughter... well, she's like a daughter, but yes she's very well thank you."

"Is she a relative?" asked John. "It's a long story," Simeon said.

"I have time, I'd love to hear it!" said John.

"Come inside, I'm about to close up." invited Simeon, "Isaac! Could you come and close up for me please lad? Thanks."

Isaac appeared out of nowhere and stared at John, recognising him instantly, "You prayed for Anna!" he exclaimed.

"This is Isaac," introduced Simeon.

"Your son?"

"In a way, yes"

"Nice to meet you, Isaac, I recognise you from before!" John patted him on the shoulder.

Simeon led John through the bakery and into his house. John sat down at the table as Simeon got him something to eat and drink.

"So, Simeon, tell me your story."

Simeon laughed, "Okay then. Well, it all started on the Day of the Feast..."

Simeon explained as best he could the events of the last few weeks, how he and Lydia had been an angry, bitter, childless couple transformed by Jesus on the Day of the Feast and were now sort of parents to Isaac and Anna. Simeon found himself feeling a little ashamed as he explained to John how he had arranged to buy a slave, but he left nothing out as John listened intently.

"That is some story!" marvelled John, "You know, being with Jesus he got to see us at our best and at our worst, but he never once judged or condemned anybody. Everything about him was love. We felt so safe with him," John's eyes twinkled, "there's no place for shame with Jesus."

Simeon found himself unable to speak with emotion as this gentle man's words were like a healing oil pouring into his heart. He nodded as tears began to flow. John put a hand on Simeon's shoulder but said nothing.

Simeon gathered himself and said with a broken voice, "We've been rescued. Sometimes I look at the change in myself and Lydia and it feels like a dream. I couldn't see it before, I couldn't even believe that God was real if I'm honest, despite my upbringing – going to temple every week - but look what he's done" Simeon gestured towards the bakery where his new family were.

John smiled, "I've heard so many stories like this, each one as precious as the next. All real! You're not dreaming!" he laughed.

They laughed together for a while and then Simeon spoke, "Actually, I could do with your advice on something."

"Okay, not sure I can help, but go ahead," replied John.

"We've sold our three extra properties and given the money away, but we also own this barn next door that we keep goats in, and for some reason we feel reluctant to sell it. We're not sure why, I'm hoping it's not because we want to hang on to it out of greed or fear. I don't think that's the reason, but this way of life, listening to the Holy Spirit and doing what he says is very new to us! And we've heard about others giving all their property away!"

John smiled at his new friend, "You have a good heart, Simeon, I don't think it's fear or greed, and Jesus knows that. I have a sense that he will tell you what to do with the barn. But now my friend, I must be on my way, the others will be getting hungry. Thanks again for the bread."

And so began a friendship between John and Simeon that they would both grow to treasure deeply.

That night Simeon told Lydia about his conversation with John, "....so, he said that Jesus would show us what to do about the barn. Has Jesus shown you anything?"

"Well, it's funny you should say that, but in my mind's eye, I just keep seeing children running around in the barn. I was wondering if that's what it should be used for, to give more homeless orphans a place to stay, what do you think?" asked Lydia.

"I like it! When you said that, it was like my heart leapt! You remember what Isaac said the other day about those children hanging around the bakery and he asked if he could feed them? Well, there must be lots of children like that, we could help them," said Simeon.

"This is so exciting! We could end up with so many children!" laughed Lydia.

A few days later at the bakery, Isaac spotted the same two boys he had seen before.

"Lydia," he called, "would you be able to take over here while I take some bread to those boys, please?"

Lydia dusted the flour off her hands and came to the large window where they sold the bread; Simeon was busy with the baking and Anna was helping him, "Sure, Isaac."

Isaac grabbed some bread and walked up to the boys, "Would you like some bread?" he asked, pushing it into their hands.

The boys grabbed the bread and ran before Isaac could even ask them their names. He was a little disappointed. He really wanted to help them.

"Give them time, Isaac, they'll be back. I'm sure you and Anna would have been suspicious of people if they'd tried to help," reassured Lydia.

"Yeah, I suppose so!"

Later that afternoon, Lydia asked Anna if she would like to take some bread round to the widow who lived just down the street. Anna said she would, so they put some bread in a basket and set off.

The widow was sitting outside her house watching the passers-by. Anna thought she looked thin and unhappy and quite scruffy. She had a sad face and an old, stained shawl that she had wrapped around her head and shoulders.

"She probably can't afford any decent clothes," Anna thought.

Lydia introduced herself and Anna to the old lady who did not offer up her own name.

The old lady eyed them suspiciously; she had seen Lydia many times and had thought she was one of the most miserable people she had ever seen. She had nicknamed her 'Sour Face'. She had never seen her with a child before.

But there was something different about Lydia, something very different! She only had to look at her face to see that an extraordinary change had taken place! Instead of the sourness was a happy, kind, soft face. She was puzzled, and still very suspicious as Lydia had never even acknowledged her before, let alone spoken to her and offered her bread which she was now doing.

The old lady was so hungry, she took the bread and began to eat, she could not afford to say no to free food. She had been a widow for several months and had no children to help her. She earnt a few coins doing bits of sewing here and there but there was not much work as most women did their own. She struggled to pay the rent for her one-roomed house and was almost at the point where she would be evicted and become homeless.

Anna was puzzled as Lydia took her by the hand and led her away, saying goodbye to the lady.

"Why aren't we staying to talk to her?" she whispered to Lydia.

"All I can say is, that I feel it would be better to get to know her a bit at a time. Just something I think the Holy Spirit is telling me," Lydia was beginning to recognise the Holy Spirit, so she obeyed the prompt she felt in her heart – she could only describe it as a feeling, no, more like a nudge in her heart.

"How did you know it was the Holy Spirit talking to you?" asked Anna. She was curious because she had heard Simeon and Lydia talk about the Holy Spirit like a friend , and she felt like she was getting to know him like that too.

"I'm not always absolutely certain. Do you remember what it felt like when the Holy Spirit spoke to you about trusting Simeon?"

"Yes."

"Well, I suppose it's a bit like that. But maybe he speaks to me in a slightly different way."

"Ah, so if I have a feeling about something that I've asked him to show me, he could be answering me?"

"Yes, for me, sometimes I would describe it like little nudges in my heart," said Lydia.

"Yes! I know what you mean!" said Anna excitedly. "So, we just have to keep doing the things the Holy Spirit tells us with this lady and see what happens?"

"I think so, yes!"

Chapter Thirteen

Leah

The next morning, after clearing up the breakfast things, Lydia and Anna collected some bread from the bakery and set off along the street.

The old lady was in her usual place, sitting outside her one-roomed house busy with some sewing.

"Morning, we've brought you some more bread," said Lydia, handing her the loaf.

"Thank you," the old lady replied suspiciously, wishing she did not need to accept it. What did they want from her? Why were they bringing food to her again? The child smiled at her but did not speak.

Lydia led Anna away again.

They did this for the next five days, just as the Holy Spirit directed them, never stopping to chat.

Then on the sixth day, something changed. As they were approaching the widow's house, they saw two men throwing her meagre belongings out onto the street, ignoring her as she pleaded with them to give her more time to pay the rent.

"Too late, lady, you're out, find somewhere else to live!" and with that, they boarded up the door so she could not get back in and left her stunned, in tears on the street.

Lydia hurried over to her, "Oh, my dear, I'm so sorry," she said to the old lady who seemed to be in shock, "why don't you come with me, and you can tell me what's happened."

The old lady allowed herself to be led away as Anna picked up her few possessions that had been thrown out onto the street.

Lydia took her into their house and made her a drink.

"What will I do?" the widow cried, "I have nowhere to go!"

Lydia took her hand and said, "If you like, you can stay here with us."

The old lady looked at her sharply, "Why would you do that for me?"

Before Lydia could answer Anna stepped in, "Because they did it for me. I was an orphan, living on the streets, me and Isaac, but they rescued us, and this is our home now, they're like our mum and dad," Anna looked at Lydia.

Lydia was astounded and fought back the tears, what had just happened? The child that she loved had just called her mum in a roundabout way! She smiled at Anna, gathered herself and spoke to the lady, "It's true, Anna here is telling the truth," she stroked Anna's hair, "we took her and Isaac in as our children; they live with us now. We met Jesus on the Day of the Feast and he changed our lives..."

The old lady whose name was Leah, listened with growing curiosity to Lydia. She found herself believing Lydia's story, maybe this was why Lydia's face had changed so dramatically. Leah had heard about this Jesus, she had heard about the goings-on on the day of the Feast, but she had stayed out of the way, too despondent to get involved in any way. But as Lydia was talking, with Anna chipping in, she began to feel hopeful, maybe her life was not over! Since she had lost her husband, she had felt so alone and hopeless, but now something was happening to her as they were speaking, something was coming alive in her!

"Would you like to know Jesus too?" asked Anna.

Leah looked at those childlike trusting eyes and knew what she needed to do, she took Anna's hands and said, "Yes please, but how do I do that?"

"What's your name?" asked Lydia.

"Leah," she replied.

"Well, Leah, you just have to believe in Jesus and what he did, it's very simple! He loves you so much, and he died so that you could be forgiven, and come home to God and know him as Father," said Lydia.

Leah sat with Lydia and Anna and asked Jesus to forgive her. The three of them prayed together and Leah was baptised in the Holy Spirit just like all of them had been.

Just then, Isaac and Simeon came in for their lunch. Simeon had hired some extra help to work in the bakery so that he could spend some more time with his new family.

Anna ran over to them and excitedly grabbed their hands, "Come and meet Leah, she loves Jesus too now, she's just asked him to forgive her!"

Simeon and Isaac were delighted and asked Leah to tell them her story. Suddenly Lydia jumped up, "I haven't prepared lunch yet!" she laughed.

"I'll help!" said Anna.

"Me too!" said Isaac.

Lydia threw Simeon a pleading look who understood straight away, "Actually, Isaac, you and I could get the plates out and lay the table, we can't have too many people preparing food." Isaac really was a disaster in the kitchen!

The five of them ate together while Leah told her story. They hid their surprise well when they learnt that she was not much older than Lydia. The passage of time had not been kind to Leah, and she looked much older than her 40 years. Leah had married at 16 and been widowed three months ago after a hard life of work and stress and very little money. She and her husband had lost their only child, a little girl who had sadly died at just a few days old.

"Well, you're very welcome to stay with us," said Simeon.

"That's so very kind of you," replied Leah, "I have absolutely nowhere else to go, no family anywhere."

"Where will Leah sleep?" Isaac asked Simeon, "We will need another bed, or she can have mine and I'll sleep in the barn or something," he offered.

"No need for that!" laughed Simeon, "we'll sort something out."

"Right, Lydia and Anna, will you please look after the bakery customers while Isaac and I make some arrangements for Leah? he asked.

"Of course," said Lydia.

"I would love to help, too," said Leah.

"That would be great, if you feel up to it," said Lydia.

As it turned out, once Leah got over her shyness, she was good with the customers. Anna was kept busy fetching and carrying and wrapping the bread that was being sold.

Suddenly they heard a loud banging coming from their barn where the goats were.

"Anna, go and see what's making that noise, I think I know what's going on, but could you just check for me please?" asked Lydia.

Anna went next door. In the barn there seemed to be at least six other people (it was difficult to be sure as they kept moving around), as well as Isaac and Simeon. They were putting up a wooden partition in the middle of the barn. Isaac came over to explain, "The goats don't need the whole barn so we're making half of it into a room for Leah. We need to repair a bit of the roof over there and put something on the floor. Joshua and his friends are making a bed, and Isaac and his sons over there, are making a table and some shelves – Simeon now calls him 'Big Isaac' to avoid confusion!"

"Where have these people come from? I don't remember seeing them before," asked Anna.

"They're all new friends of Simeon."

"And they're all happy to help?"

"Yep, free of charge, cos that's what families do!"

Anna thought about it, "I suppose if we're all God's children then we're brothers and sisters, like one big family."

"Yep!"

"Wow! Leah is going to have a huge room! Why didn't they make it smaller?"

"Big Isaac asked Simeon about that, and Simeon said God told him Leah would need a large space. And you remember what Simeon and Lydia said the other day about using the barn to house homeless children." said Isaac.

Anna shuddered as she remembered what it was like to be homeless, scared, and hungry, "Isaac, wouldn't it be amazing if we could help all those children!"

Anna went back into the bakery to tell Lydia about Simeon's plans.

Lydia smiled as Joshua and Big Isaac's wives had already told her what their husbands were doing, when they had brought some clothes over for Leah, and a straw mattress to go on the bed that Joshua was making.

By the end of the day, the barn looked thoroughly respectable! The cleaned stone floor had some rugs spread on it, there was a little table and some shelves, and a wooden bed with the straw mattress in the corner with a cosy woollen blanket.

"Oh my!" cried Leah when she saw it, "I've never slept on a bed before! Thank you so much!"

That night, Simeon and Lydia talked about their day, "So I thought Leah could be the first of many to stay in the barn," said Simeon, "maybe she could help look after any children that we rescue. We might even find whole families that need somewhere to stay, that barn is so big!"

"I think it's a wonderful idea," agreed Lydia, "Oh, I'd almost forgotten, when Anna was talking to Leah about us, she said 'they are like my mum and dad' isn't that wonderful? I would love her and Isaac to call me 'mum', do you think they ever will?"

"Maybe, in their own time they will," replied Simeon.

Chapter Fourteen

Rescuers

Isaac was enjoying his new life, but he could not forget how scared he had felt on the streets and how hungry and cold he had been at times. He really wanted to rescue other children who were homeless. He knew there were plenty of children out there in danger and he wanted to help them. He had talked his idea through with Simeon, and they had decided that the children were more likely to trust Isaac if he was on his own.

A few days later, as he walked around the city, he prayed, "Jesus, please help me find the children who you want me to rescue."

Eventually he came across the two young boys that he recognised from outside the bakery. They did not recognise him at first but as he started to chat to them and offered them some of the bread he had taken with him, they realised who he was, "I know you," said the bigger of the two, "you've given us bread before, you work at that bakery."

"Yes, I'm Isaac, what are your names?"

"I'm Matthew and this is Joel," the larger boy replied.

"Where do you live?" asked Isaac.

"We live on the streets," said Matthew.

"I used to live on the streets too, but not anymore," said Isaac.

"What happened? Where do you live now?" asked Joel in a small voice.

Isaac told his story. The boys listened, "Come with me and I'll show you where I live," said Isaac.

Joel's eyes lit up, but Matthew looked suspicious.

"Wait..." Matthew put his hand on Joel's arm and looked at Isaac, "how can we trust you?"

"You already know where I live, just come and visit sometime and you can have some more bread." Isaac desperately wanted to invite the boys home with him there and then, they were both younger than Isaac and he was sure the smaller one, Joel, was younger than Anna, but he was beginning to recognise those little prompts from the Holy Spirit that Lydia talked about, and he felt one of those nudges right now that said, 'walk away.'

So, he did.

Nevertheless, he was struggling with doubts when he got home, "What if I walked away too soon? What if I didn't hear the Holy Spirit right?" he worried to Lydia.

"Isaac, love, God cares about those two boys even more than you or I do. He can take care of them. Look how he brought you two to us. No-one could have dreamt how that would happen. Come on, let's ask him to protect those two young lads." reassured Lydia.

Isaac did not see Matthew and Joel for a whole week. He kept looking out for them and giving away bread to hungry children, just trying to make friends.

Isaac was helping in the bakery when he spotted Matthew and Joel across the street, "Simeon, could I go out for a minute? I've just seen Matthew and Joel."

"Of course!"

Isaac went across the street, and walked up to the two boys, "Hi Matthew, hi Joel," he said.

"Hello," replied Matthew.

"So, how's it going?" Isaac asked. Joel raised his head and Isaac saw that his eye was bruised and swollen.

Neither boy seemed to know what to say to Isaac. They clearly wanted to talk but were finding it difficult to know where to begin.

"What happened to your eye?" asked Isaac, "Did someone hit you?" Joel just shrugged.

"It's no fun living on the streets! Did you get that begging?" Joel looked down at his feet.

"It happened to me a few times," said Isaac. He could see the pain in Matthew's eyes, he knew how Matthew felt, there were times when he had not been able to protect Anna and it had felt awful, "would you like to come inside the bakery and see where I live?" he asked.

Both boys nodded shyly, so Isaac led them into the bakery. He called to Simeon, "Is it okay if I just take my friends into the house?"

Simeon looked up and smiled at Matthew and Joel, "Of course," he said.

Matthew and Joel kept looking around, trying to take in the size of the house and all its furniture. Isaac took them upstairs.

"You have an upstairs?" exclaimed Joel, his eyes wide.

"Wow!" said Matthew, "You even have proper beds with mattresses and a rug on the floor!"

"Yes, life has really changed for me. We have a big barn next door as well, with a room for you if you want it, you don't have to go back out on the streets, you can stay with us."

Joel looked pleadingly at Matthew; he desperately wanted a safe place of their own.

Isaac continued, "we can feed you; we have meat and vegetables and honey and figs and goat's milk and Lydia is a brilliant cook!"

"Isaac, are you sure? What do we have to do?" asked Matthew.

Isaac looked him directly in the eye and said, "Nothing! Just come back downstairs and meet my family," it still gave Isaac such a thrill to be able to call them that.

All three boys went downstairs to the kitchen where Lydia, Anna and Leah were preparing lunch.

Isaac introduced his new friends. "Hi," said Anna shyly, smiling.

"Lovely to meet you, Matthew and Joel. Would you like to have some lunch with us?" asked Lydia.

"Joel," said Leah, "would you like me to put something on that eye? It looks very sore."

Joel looked at Matthew asking for his permission and when Matthew nodded, he moved slowly over to Leah.

Lydia watched Leah with Joel and saw how natural she was with him, and how comfortable Joel was with Leah.

When Simeon came in for lunch, Anna noticed how Matthew and Joel both tensed when they saw him. She remembered how scared she had been of Simeon; after all he could appear large and intimidating to those who did not know him. To break the tension, Anna rushed over to him, and he picked her up and swung her in the air.

"Hello, sweetheart," he said, kissing her on the cheek.

"Simeon, this is Matthew and Joel," she said, pointing at the two boys.

Simeon put Anna down and smiled at them, "Hello Matthew and Joel, welcome to our home. Are you staying for lunch?"

Both boys nodded, feeling a little afraid, but they relaxed when

Simeon patted them on their shoulders and said, "Excellent, what a treat!"

They all sat down at the table together. It was a large table and Simeon had bought more chairs and stools since they had been having lots of people round for meals lately. Matthew and Joel ate greedily and messily, they did not join in the conversation, and no-one made them. Isaac, Anna, and Leah still remembered what it was like to be hungry.

At the end of the meal, Matthew and Joel sat back holding their stomachs; never before had they eaten so much in one meal!

"Well, I need to get back to work," said Simeon reluctantly. He would have liked to spend time with the two boys, but he knew that they would probably talk more if they were with the children.

"I'll come and help you," said Lydia, "Are you okay to clear up, Leah?"

"Of course," said Leah, "I'm sure I have some willing helpers here."

Isaac groaned, and Anna gave him a sharp look, "Yes, we'll help," she said.

"I could help as well," said Matthew.

"Excellent! No, Joel, you sit down," Leah said as Joel got up to help, "you look really tired, why don't you curl up in that big chair in the corner and have a rest?"

Again, Joel looked to Matthew for permission and having got the nod from him, went to sit in the big comfy chair in the corner.

As the children helped Leah clear up, Isaac noticed Matthew constantly glancing across at Joel, "He's very protective of him," he thought. When Joel fell asleep after a short while, Matthew seemed to relax a bit.

"Are you brothers?" Anna asked him.

"Yes," said Matthew. He was not a great conversationalist, Isaac thought, but if anyone could get him talking it would be Anna.

"How old are you?" she asked.

"I'm eleven, he's seven."

"How long have you been on your own?"

"Er... not sure really. Probably over a year."

"Wow! That's a long time. What happened to your parents?" asked Isaac.

Matthew had never talked to anyone about his parents, but somehow, he felt able to with Isaac and Anna, "There was a fight in our village with some Roman soldiers. Our parents were killed, lots of people were killed. Some of the other children were taken as slaves but I ran away with Joel. We ended up in Jerusalem. It's easier to hide here and beg for food."

"That's horrible," said Anna, "you must have been so frightened!"

Matthew shrugged and tried to put on a brave face, "Well Joel was, but I had to look after him."

"You poor boys, so young to be on your own!" said Leah putting her arm around Matthew and feeling how thin he was. She felt a rush of affection for these boys who had been through so much and felt an overwhelming desire to care for them.

Matthew was struggling to cope with such kindness.

"Well, you can stay with us now," said Anna, "we've got plenty of room haven't we Leah?"

"Absolutely, that barn is too big for me on my own and I could do with some company, so you'd really be doing me a favour if you stayed."

Isaac realised that Leah was making it easier for Matthew to receive their help.

Matthew hesitated for a moment and looked across the room at Joel asleep in the big comfortable chair. He made his decision, "Okay, thank you," he said.

"Good, that's sorted then. Isaac, could you go and tell Simeon and Lydia so that we can sort out a couple of mattresses for the boys, please?" said Leah.

Isaac was so excited when he went into the bakery, "Simeon! They said they'd stay! That's our first lot of children! I'm going to go out and get some more!"

"Hold on!" laughed Simeon, "Let's get these two settled first, then you can go hunting for more! Now, go to Big Isaac's house and let him know we need two more beds and mattresses; he said he would make some for us."

Isaac ran out of the bakery and along the street to Big Isaac's house. He had been there once before with Simeon so knew where he lived.

Big Isaac was a carpenter. He was not particularly big at all, but the name he was given the day they worked in the barn, had stuck. He and his family lived in a small house with a workshop attached where Big Isaac worked, and people came to buy his wooden creations.

"Well, hello there, Small Isaac!" greeted Big Isaac.

"You'll never guess what? We've got two boys who are going to stay with Leah in the barn. We rescued them off the streets, they're orphans like me and Anna, and I've been wanting to help them for a while, but I had to wait because God told me to and then they came to the bakery! But Matthew, the older one – although he's younger than me – didn't want to admit that they needed help so Leah made out it was a favour to her, and he said yes, and his younger brother Joel will do whatever Matthew says, so they're staying with us! Isn't that great?"

Big Isaac laughed at the torrent of words coming from Isaac, "That's wonderful! It just so happens that I've just finished making two of the beds I promised Simeon. I'll get the mattresses ready and bring them over this evening just before dinner."

"Excellent!" shouted Isaac as he ran out of the door, racing to get back to his two new friends.

Big Isaac chuckled to himself as he watched Isaac run up the street. He remembered the first time he had seen Isaac, just a few days after Simeon had bought him; he was all skin and bone then with big shadows under his eyes and a haunted look. What a transformation! Isaac had thickened out, his hair was shiny, his eyes were bright, and he had grown quite a bit! He wondered how long it would be before they had to swap their nicknames and he would become the small Isaac!

When Isaac got back, he found Anna showing Matthew around the barn.

"So, it's just like a house now," Anna was telling him, "lots of friends came round to help change it all when Leah came to stay, and we want more children to come and be safe here."

Matthew was puzzled. What was it about these people that made them so kind and generous? There was something different about them, "Why do you do all this?" he asked.

"I remember what it was like to be an orphan. Simeon and Lydia rescued us and gave us a home, and it's all because of Jesus!" chipped in Isaac.

Matthew turned around; he had not heard Isaac come in.

"I remember you mentioning that name before. Are you talking about that Jesus who was crucified by the Romans? I thought he was dead."

"He came alive again!" said Anna.

"No, I saw him die! I watched him being nailed to a cross. I had to cover Joel's eyes, it was horrible, but I couldn't leave. It went dark, then the sun came out again and I watched a soldier check to see if he was dead by sticking a spear in him, then someone came and took his body away. I saw it, there is no way he is alive!" protested Matthew.

"That's true," explained Anna, "we were there too, we were so upset, but he came alive again. A lot of people saw him."

"Did you see him?"

"No, but we know he did."

"How do you know?"

Isaac and Anna sat down with Matthew and told their story from beginning to end and spoke of how Jesus had changed Simeon and Lydia too.

"I can't believe that a dead man could come alive again. I just don't think it's possible." said Matthew.

Just then, Leah came into the barn with a frightened Joel who had woken up and panicked at not seeing Matthew.

"It's ok Joel, I'm here, I won't leave you," comforted Matthew as Joel clung on to him. "This is where we're going to sleep tonight, we've got two real beds coming with mattresses!"

"Yes, and I'll be over there in my bed, so if you need anything or feel afraid, I'll be right here." said Leah.

Leah left the children to chat with one another in the barn and went to the bakery to see Simeon and Lydia.

"How are Matthew and Joel?" asked Lydia.

"They'll be fine, Isaac and Anna are looking after them and they're starting to relax a bit now."

"Are you sure you're okay with them being with you in the barn?" asked Lydia.

Leah laughed, "Just you try and stop me! A warm comfortable bed and children to mother, what more could I want?"

Lydia smiled and hugged her, "I'm so glad you came into our lives."

"Now, now, don't get me started," said Leah wiping away a tear.

That evening the number of people eating dinner was even greater than at midday, Big Isaac, his family, and another friend called James had joined them. There was laughter and storytelling and praying and worshipping, something they often did when they got together. Matthew and Joel were amazed at the sense of family. They all kept talking about this Jesus as if he really was alive!

Joel sidled up to Anna and said, "You believe in Jesus, don't you?"

Anna nodded.

"Can I talk to him like you do?" Joel asked.

"Of course you can," said Anna and introduced him to Jesus just as she had Leah.

In the meantime, Matthew was in conversation with Isaac and Simeon, "How can you know this Jesus is alive if you can't actually see him?" he asked.

"Would it be alright if we asked Jesus to show you?" asked Simeon.

Matthew nodded and Simeon and Isaac placed their hands gently on his shoulders and prayed. Suddenly they noticed tears rolling down Matthew's cheeks.

"What's happening Matthew?" asked Isaac.

"He's real! I know he's real! Jesus, I love you!" whispered Matthew.

Isaac was astounded! He looked at Simeon, "I like introducing people to Jesus!" he whispered.

"Me too!" said Simeon.

Chapter Fifteen

Family

That night Matthew and Joel slept deeper and longer than they had for many months. Leah woke them in the morning with a cup of fresh goat's milk, "Morning boys!" she smiled, "You've been asleep for a long time, so I thought I'd better wake you, I know you wouldn't want to miss breakfast."

"We get breakfast?" asked Joel.

Leah laughed, "Of course you do!"

"Can we stay here tonight as well?" Joel asked.

"Joel, this is your home for as long as you want it. This is your bed, this is your blanket, this is your room that you share with me and Matthew and any other children that need it."

Matthew grinned at Joel remembering the night before, "It's all real Joel!" he reassured his younger brother.

Isaac and Anna were waiting in the kitchen for Matthew and Joel. Anna was looking forward to their first breakfast together.

Both Matthew and Joel looked startled at the amount of food on the table. Freshly baked bread, warm from the oven, ripe figs and delicious sweet honey this morning. Matthew could not remember eating like this even when his parents had been alive.

"I can't believe you eat like this," Matthew looked at Isaac, "there's so much food!"

Isaac laughed, "I know, I felt the same when I first came here!"

They ate in relative silence, that is, apart from the noise of four hungry children enjoying a delicious breakfast. Leah smiled as she watched them.

"What are you up to today?" Anna asked Isaac.

"I thought I'd go out to look for more children," said Isaac.

"It would be nice to have some more girls around here, I'm starting to feel a bit outnumbered!"

"Why don't you come with me then? You know I'll keep you safe, I always did before."

"I don't know..."

"I'll come...if you want me to," said Matthew hesitantly.

"That would be great!" replied Isaac, "Come on Anna, please."

"I don't know, let me talk to Lydia first."

Joel was looking a bit worried; he did not want to go out on the streets again yet.

"Joel, would you like to stay with me? I could do with some help today, and Simeon could always use some help in the bakery." said Leah.

Joel nodded in relief, he felt safe with Leah.

Anna went next door to the bakery, "Hello sweetheart," greeted Lydia.

"Isaac asked if I could go out with him today to look for more children. I want to go but I'm a bit scared, I've not been out without you or Simeon since I came here, but I want to go, and Matthew said he would come too."

"Anna, I know you're a bit scared, but you know Isaac will look after you and I trust God to look after all of you. Just stick together, all three of you."

Anna nodded and ran back to the kitchen. She felt comforted knowing she was going with Isaac and Matthew, and she knew Jesus would look after them, "Okay, I'm coming, but you have to stay with me." she said to Isaac.

They set off carrying plenty of bread to give away. Isaac and Matthew between them knew many of the places they were likely to find the children who lived on the streets. That day they met a total of seven children. Three of them were orphans and the other four were out on the streets begging, as their parents were so poor they could not afford to feed them.

Isaac gave them all bread and told them that there would always be food for them at the bakery. However, all but one of the children had run off after taking the bread before he could tell them where the bakery was.

One little girl had stayed after taking the bread. She had not spoken at all, and she looked desperately hungry and tired. Anna bent down to look her in the eyes and said, "Hi, my name's Anna what's yours?"

The little girl met her eyes but would not answer. "Do you have a mum and dad?" asked Isaac.

The little girl shook her head.

"Would you like to come back to our home and have some food and somewhere safe and warm to sleep?" asked Anna gently. The little girl stared at them with tired, empty eyes and nodded vacantly, so Anna held out her hand and the little girl took it shyly.

It took an hour to get back home as the little girl was clearly exhausted and unable to walk at Anna, Isaac, and Matthew's pace.

"Should I carry her?" whispered Isaac whose muscles were beginning to develop from his work in the bakery lifting sacks of flour.

"No," whispered back Anna, "I think it will frighten her, let's just take our time".

Eventually, they arrived back at the bakery and were met by Leah, "Well, who do we have here?" she smiled.

"We don't know her name, all we know is she's an orphan and she lives on the streets," explained Anna.

Leah sat down on a stool so she could look the child in her eyes, "You look so tired sweetie, why don't you come in and sit down and you can have some milk to drink?"

The children were happy to leave the little girl with Leah as she was clearly exhausted and overwhelmed. They went to find Joel; he was in the bakery with Simeon and Lydia. Simeon had given him a small brush and he was vainly attempting to sweep the floor, "I'm helping!" he cried when he saw them.

"Yes you are!" said Simeon smiling and patting him on the shoulder as Joel beamed with pride.

"So, how did you three get on?" asked Lydia.

"We met seven children, but only one little girl came back with us, she's with Leah right now. We tried to tell the others where we live so they could come and get food, but they ran off too quickly. Not all of them were orphans though, some of them were just out begging because they don't have enough food at home," replied Isaac.

"You sound a little disappointed," said Lydia.

"Yes, I wanted them to trust us. They could have so much more here with us!"

"Don't worry, these things take time." Lydia reassured him.

Meanwhile, in the kitchen, Leah had put some vegetable stew in front of the little girl who had still not spoken a word and seemed afraid to eat the food.

"It's alright," Leah said, "this is for you, you can eat it."

The child was so hungry, after only a moment's hesitation, she tucked into the delicious stew. Leah watched and smiled as the little girl licked her plate clean. Leah poured her a drink of goat's milk and sat down at the table, "Can you tell me your name?" she asked.

The child looked up into Leah's kindly eyes and whispered, "Rebekah".

"That's a lovely name, how old are you, Rebekah?"

"Six, I think."

"Only six!" said Leah, "and what about your mum and dad?" Rebekah just shook her head and tears filled her eyes.

"That's alright," soothed Leah, "you can tell me about them another day. You look tired; would you like to sit in that chair in the corner while I prepare dinner for this evening?"

Leah chatted away to Rebekah while she worked, sneaking a glance at her every so often just to keep an eye on her. After a short while she noticed Rebekah had fallen fast asleep.

At that moment, Lydia came in, "How is she?" she whispered noticing Rebekah asleep in the chair.

"Poor love, she was starving and exhausted. Her name's Rebekah, she's six and she's an orphan, but that's all I could get out of her. She seems really scared, not that I can blame her!" said Leah.

"Oh Leah, I think we're going to be finding quite a few Rebekah's!" said Lydia.

"Yes, and we can give them all a home!"

Lydia smiled inwardly at the change in Leah, she looked as if the years had fallen off her, she was no longer stooped, and she seemed happier and more confident.

"I thought my life was over, but I'm loving every minute of it now, I cannot express how grateful I am to you and Simeon, and to God, for rescuing me!"

Smiling, Lydia stepped forward and gave Leah a big hug.

It took a few days for Rebekah to settle in and not be startled every time she heard a loud noise. Over time, her story came out. She and her sister had fled from their home, just outside the city, when their mother had become ill and died. Their father had died only a few months before their mother, she was not sure how, she just remembered being told the sad news.

Rebekah had become separated from her older sister a week or so ago and had tried unsuccessfully to fend for herself, and as a result had become starved, cold, and exhausted. She had been unable to find her sister and was terrified that she had been taken by slave traders.

Isaac, when he had heard Rebekah's story had promised to look for her sister when he was out looking for other orphans. This had sparked hope in Rebekah's eyes and that hope grew in her heart when she came to know Jesus.

Isaac, Anna, and Matthew were now going out most days looking for lost, orphaned, hungry, or unwanted children. By now, they had six children staying in the barn with Leah, who was revelling in her role as mother. Leah and Lydia were busy with all the cooking and baking and making clothes for the children. Friends and neighbours were contributing beds, mattresses, and blankets.

One night, as Simeon and Lydia were getting ready for bed, Lydia said, "We're going to run out of room soon, and I cannot face the thought of turning a child away! What shall we do?"

Simeon yawned and said, "Actually, a number of our friends have already approached me, offering to take some of the children in and give them a home, like we did with Isaac and Anna. What do you think?"

"Oh Simeon, wouldn't it be wonderful, to be able to give these children a new family!"

The next morning, they told Leah their plan.

"I know it's the right thing to do, but it will be hard to let them go. And I've been thinking about Rebekah, I would like to adopt her as mine and her sister when we find her. What do you think?"

"Oh Leah, that would be wonderful!"

And so it happened. Many believers, having been changed by God's love, were more than willing to adopt the children. Simeon and Lydia made sure that brothers and sisters were kept together. It was hard for Isaac and Anna when Matthew and Joel were adopted as they had become firm friends. But, as all the children were in and out of each other's houses regularly, they quickly adjusted to the new arrangement.

Chapter Sixteen

Babies

One day, Isaac and Anna were out on their own, Matthew and Joel were travelling with their parents to meet their new aunts, uncles, and cousins. Isaac and Anna went further afield than they had done before and came across a young girl with a crying baby. The girl was as distressed as the baby.

"What's wrong?" asked Anna, putting her hand on the girl's arm.

"I just want him to stop crying, I don't know what to do! I think he's hungry, but I can't feed him! I wrapped him up in this shawl that I have, so I don't think he's cold but..."

"Where's his mother? Your mother I assume?" asked Isaac.

"I don't know, he's not my brother. I don't have a mother, I found him, and I couldn't leave him! They just left him out there to die, I couldn't let that happen, but I don't know what to do!" the girl looked desperately at Isaac and Anna, "What do I do?"

Anna was puzzled by the girl's words, "I don't understand, what do you mean, 'left there'…" she began, but the girl was too distressed to answer. Anna looked to Isaac who just shrugged, clearly, he didn't understand what the girl was trying to say any more than Anna did.

"What's your name?" asked Anna.

"Hannah."

"I'm Anna, and this is Isaac."

"And what's his name?" asked Isaac, pointing to the baby.

"I don't know."

Isaac and Anna looked confused, "Okay, start from the beginning. Why do you have this baby whose name you don't know?" asked Isaac.

Hannah rocked the crying baby in her arms as she tried to explain, but as the baby's cries became louder, they could not hear a word she was saying.

Isaac beckoned to Hannah, "Give him to me".

Hannah, desperate for any help, handed the crying baby to Isaac. As he took the baby wrapped in the shawl, Isaac was surprised at how tiny he was, and saw a small, withered hand poking out from the shawl. He held him to his chest and prayed, "Jesus, please make him quiet so we can talk."

Hannah looked on in astonishment as the baby quietened and fell asleep. "How did you do that?" she asked.

"Wasn't me, Jesus did it."

"Jesus who?"

"I'll explain later, tell us your story."

They found a wall to sit on and Hannah began to explain, "I was walking just outside the city looking for my sister, when I saw this Roman soldier putting this bundle of what I thought were rags on the ground in some rocks, and just walking away. I didn't think anything of it until I overheard some women saying that it was another Roman baby being exposed. I didn't understand what they were talking about, but one woman was saying that if the father thinks there's something wrong with the baby, he just leaves it out to die. Well, I couldn't let that happen so when the women had gone, I went to the bundle and found this little one crying his eyes out, and as you can see, he has something wrong with his arm."

"That's awful!" shrieked Anna, "How could anyone do that to a baby? Are you going to take him home with you?" she asked Hannah.

"I don't have a home," mumbled Hannah sadly, "but I couldn't leave him to die, although he probably will because I can't feed him!"

Anna turned to Isaac, "We have to take Hannah and this baby home with us."

"Agreed. Hannah, come with us, it's quite a way, but we can give you food and a place to stay and something for this little chap."

Hannah was unsure, but she had no choice. She felt so protective towards the baby, and she knew she could not look after him on her own. As they walked back, she told them her story, "My sister and I had to leave home when our mum died. Our dad had died a few months before, so we had no-one to look after us. We have relatives somewhere, but I don't know how to find them. My sister and I got separated and I've been looking for her ever since, but it's been over a week now and I'm so scared that she's been taken by slave traders, she's only six!"

Isaac and Anna's eyes brightened, and they looked at each other asking at the same time, "What's her name?"

Hannah was a little taken aback, "Er... Rebekah. Why?"

"What does she look like?" they both said at the same time.

"Well, she's about this big," Hannah held her hand midway between her waist and shoulders "and she has brown curly hair and brown eyes and she's wearing a blue tunic and she's barefoot..."

Isaac was about to tell Hannah that they had Rebekah but was stopped short by a dig in the ribs from Anna and an almost imperceptible shake of her head. He looked at her as she spoke quietly out of the corner of her mouth, "Just in case it's not her".

Isaac nodded and turned to Hannah, "Almost there!" he said.

As they got to their house, Hannah hesitated to go in but followed Isaac since he was still carrying the baby, and she was not going to let him out of her sight. Leah turned around with a welcoming smile as she heard them come in. Rebekah, who was helping Leah, turned around too, and let out a squeal of delight as she saw her big sister! Hannah was stunned as Rebekah threw herself at her. Both sisters began speaking at once as they clung on to one another.

Anna hastily explained about Rebekah and Hannah to Leah. In the chaos of the reunion, it took Leah a few moments to notice the baby that Isaac was holding.

Wiping tears of joy from her eyes she looked at Isaac, "Who have you got there, Isaac?" she asked. Isaac explained what had happened as Leah took the baby from him.

Just then Simeon and Lydia rushed in from the bakery to see what all the commotion was about. They were utterly delighted when they heard all the details. Leah handed Lydia the baby so that she could take care of Hannah and give her some food.

"We need to give this little chap some milk," said Lydia as the baby started to stir.

"We need a nursing mother, someone who's got a baby who wouldn't mind feeding another one," said Leah who had just put a plate of food in front of Hannah, "I'll be back shortly!" and she raced out of the door.

A short while later she came back with a young woman called Deborah who they all knew; she had a small baby, just three months old. Deborah took the baby from Lydia, "Well, hello my little man!" she smiled. Simeon and Isaac went back into the bakery so Deborah could feed the baby in peace. He drank hungrily as Hannah explained how she had found him abandoned.

"How could anyone abandon a baby like that?" cried Deborah, "I think I'll have to take him home with me so that I can feed him through the night, I'm just so glad that my little Elijah sleeps well."

"But what about me, can't I do anything?" said Hannah, one arm still wrapped around Rebekah while she ate. She was relieved that the adults were taking charge, but she still felt protective towards this baby that she had rescued.

"You could bring him over here anytime and that way, Hannah could still get to see him." suggested Leah.

"So, does he have a name?" asked Deborah. They all looked at Hannah who shrugged.

"I think Hannah should name him," said Anna, "as she found him". Everyone agreed.

"Micah," proclaimed Hannah, "that was our dad's name," she said with tears in her eyes.

Leah put her arm round Hannah, "That's a beautiful name for a beautiful baby."

Just then, Jeremiah, Deborah's husband, came in carrying Elijah.

"Simeon said I'd find you in here. How's the baby, and where did he come from?" he asked, allowing Lydia to take Elijah from him for a cuddle.

They relayed the story and when they spoke about Micah's deformed arm, Jeremiah pulled back the shawl that was covering him and had a look, "I saw Jesus heal a withered hand once..." he began.

"So did I!" interrupted Anna in excitement, "That's what we should do!"

Jeremiah chuckled, "Come on then Anna, come and pray with me."

They put their hands on Micah's arm while he was still feeding, and simply prayed, "In the name of Jesus be healed!"

Anna felt the movement beneath her hand before she saw it. She gasped as she took her hand away to find a perfectly formed arm! Everyone was speechless, which was a good thing as Micah had just fallen into a peaceful sleep and no-one wanted to wake him. Silent tears ran down the faces of Leah and Lydia, "Look what you did Hannah, look what Jesus has done!" said Leah as she turned to Hannah and Rebekah, "God bless you for rescuing this little chap!"

Hannah, who had tears in her eyes, suddenly felt exhausted. She had been so worried about what to do with this baby, and how to find Rebekah and now she was in a house with grown- ups who could take charge and Rebekah and Micah were both safe.

Leah, seeing Hannah overcome with weariness, led her to the big chair in the corner and told her to rest for a while, as they cleared up, then she would show her where she was going to sleep that night - in a bed right next to Rebekah.

Deborah became a regular visitor with her two babies, she and Jeremiah had decided to raise Micah as their own as a brother for Elijah.

A few days after Micah had been found, Isaac and Anna were talking with Hannah, "What if there are more babies like Micah being abandoned? They will need rescuing as well!" said Anna.

"Yes, but how are we going to be able to look out for those babies as well as look for other older children to rescue?" asked Isaac.

"I don't know," worried Anna, realising that they could not be everywhere at once and they would certainly not be allowed out on their own at night which they thought would be the most likely time for a baby to be abandoned. Hannah, who had also come to know Jesus said, "We could always ask Jesus to show us".

So, they did, "Jesus, please show us what to do," Isaac asked.

"You know, I think we need to ask the adults, we need their help!" said Anna. They all agreed.

"Why don't we ask Jeremiah?" said Hannah.

"Yes," said Anna, "I just got one of those 'heart nudges' as Lydia calls them, when you said that."

That evening when Jeremiah called round, to have some food with his family, the children spoke to him, "So, we were praying, and we felt that we should speak to you about it," explained Isaac as he told Jeremiah of their concerns about the abandoned babies.

Jeremiah chuckled, "Funny you should say that, I've been talking to some friends, and we've all agreed to take it in turns to go to the place you found Micah and keep a look out. I've got so many volunteers; we can be there day and night! But I need you to show me exactly where it is."

"We will!" yelled all three together in excitement. "Let's go now!" said Isaac.

"Hold on," interrupted Lydia, "it's dark, how will you find the place?"

"I know exactly where it is, Hannah explained it to me." replied Isaac.

"I'm coming too," said Simeon, "right after we've all eaten."

They ate, enjoying Lydia's cooking and then Isaac, Simeon and Jeremiah set off. Hannah had protested a little, and Anna had protested a lot about not being allowed to go.

"It's not fair! I want to go!" she had pleaded but to no avail. She was about to argue some more but after a stern look from Simeon, she backed down knowing she would not win that argument. Anna rather sulkily helped Lydia and Leah clear up after the meal.

"Right then, girls, bedtime!" said Leah to Hannah and Rebekah. She got no argument from them because they were still tired after their ordeal.

Deborah had taken her babies home and only Lydia and Anna were left in the kitchen, "Right, bed for you, young lady!" said Lydia.

Anna did not want to go, what if the men came back with a baby? She said as much to Lydia.

"I think, there are going to be many more rescued babies and children and even some adults like Leah and you can't stay awake for all of them! I know you don't understand Anna, but I need you to trust me. You need your sleep; you are only ten years old!" replied Lydia.

"But what about Isaac? Why does he get to go?"

"Because he knows the way and he's older than you!"

"But..."

"Anna, you really need to go to bed!" said Lydia firmly.

"Okay," Anna gave in and allowed Lydia to take her up to bed. "Can you tell me a story please?" asked Anna.

"Of course, I'll tell you a story that my mother used to tell me, it's one of my favourites..." Anna had fallen asleep when Lydia was only half-way through the story.

Isaac, Simeon, and Jeremiah in the meantime, had found the place where Micah had been abandoned. They were hiding behind some large boulders because there was a man walking towards them. They held their breath and watched but he walked straight past them. "It might take a long time before we find any more babies," said Jeremiah, "You know what, why don't you two get back, I think I'll take first watch tonight," he offered.

Isaac and Simeon reluctantly left Jeremiah there and returned home. It took less than an hour for two fit young men!

For twenty-four hours a day after that first watch, there was always someone there. People had volunteered freely to take it in turns to watch in pairs so that if a baby were rescued, one could take him or her back while the other one stayed to keep watch for anymore and with over forty volunteers, it was not too taxing.

For two weeks they kept watch, but no more babies were abandoned. "Are we missing them do you think?" asked Anna.

"No, love. If you think about it, most babies are born healthy and are kept by their parents. It wouldn't be a problem if we kept watch for a whole year and only rescued one baby!" said Lydia.

Simeon looked at Lydia thoughtfully. "Do you still want a baby?" he asked her quietly, out of earshot of the children.

Lydia smiled "You know, I feel like now we have our children. I love Isaac and Anna so much; I don't feel like anything's missing anymore. What about you?"

"I feel the same as you. We already have our children. But you know, I wonder if we could make it official."

"What do you mean?"

"Well, adopt them formally, a bit like the Romans do. As if they had been ours by birth and so they would have an inheritance," replied Simeon.

"Oh Simeon, that would be wonderful! But how do we do that? I mean, it's not something us Jews do, is it?"

"Not normally, but you know John often talks about God adopting us and making us his children. Let me have a think about it. Shall we tell the children? Or even ask them?"

"No," laughed Lydia, "let's surprise them!"

"Good idea," said Simeon hugging his wife.

Chapter Seventeen

Adoption

A week later, Simeon and Lydia decided to have a celebration, a gathering of their new friends and family. They had to be careful because although they had not yet personally experienced trouble from the religious authorities, friends had been arrested and flogged for following Jesus.

They had cleared as much space as they could in the barn. There was plenty of food and wine and the children found it all extremely exciting running around with their friends. Matthew and Joel were there looking well fed and happy as were the other children that had been taken in by families.

About halfway through the evening, John (the apostle and good friend of Simeon and Lydia) stood up and got everyone's attention.

"Brothers and sisters, it's great to be able to come together and celebrate Simeon's plan." The adults were all smiling knowingly. Isaac and Anna looked at one another, puzzled, as did most of the other children. John continued, "The work done here has caused me great joy. It has been remarkable to see so many lives changed, so many children rescued and placed in families and all because of what Jesus has done for us. But tonight, we want to honour and recognise the love that has been expressed by you all. Children, you who were orphans have now been placed in families, given new mums and dads and brothers and sisters." He looked at the children, who had all gathered, and smiled at them, "Your new parents wanted to do something to celebrate adopting you as their own, so we decided to have this special evening together, and I have some pieces of parchment here for each new family to mark this wonderful occasion."

"So, new parents, if you could all find your children, I'd like to hand these out." Everyone shuffled around finding their families. Isaac and Anna looked at one another with wide eyes, they had not suspected a thing!

"Right," continued John, "I'd like to start with Isaac and Anna who tonight are being adopted by Simeon and Lydia."

Simeon got down on one knee in front of the children so he could look them in the eyes and said, "Isaac and Anna, you have brought us so much joy. Lydia and I love you with all our hearts and we would like to adopt you as our children and be your mum and dad."

Isaac and Anna could only nod and throw themselves into Simeon's arms as they wept tears of joy. Lydia got down on her knees too as both children then hugged her. There was not a dry eye in the place. John handed Isaac the piece of parchment that he had signed and sealed with some wax.

This happy scene was repeated many times as children were adopted into their new families. What a celebration they had afterwards!

At one point, Anna found herself talking to John, "Do you think Jesus is pleased that we've been adopted?" she asked him.

John laughed, "Anna, I think the whole of Heaven is rejoicing at this moment! Do you know, there was one time when parents kept bringing their children to Jesus so he could put his hands on them and bless them, and we tried to stop them. We kept telling these people that Jesus was too busy, too important to bother with children. And do you know what Jesus said to us?"

Anna nodded in excitement, "I was there!" she said, "but I don't remember exactly what he said."

"He told us off! He said children were just as important as grown ups and we were never to stop them coming to him again! I know how precious you are to him, and I know he's delighted that you're in a family!" John's eyes twinkled as he affectionately ruffled Anna's hair. She grinned up at him and ran off to find Isaac.

Isaac was playing with Matthew, as Anna interrupted him, "What is it?" he asked.

"Do you think we can call Simeon and Lydia mum and dad now?" Anna asked.

"I guess so, shall we ask them?"

The children found Simeon and Lydia, and Isaac, suddenly feeling a little awkward asked them, "Do you think, I mean would it be alright if..."

"Can we call you mum and dad now?" interrupted Anna impatiently.

"Of course you can sweetheart!" said Lydia with a catch in her voice. Simeon was unable to speak, he just nodded and brushed away his tears as he hugged both of his children.

Simeon and Lydia looked at one another after the children had run off to play with their friends. They grasped one another's hands, words were not necessary as they watched their son and daughter playing, seeing the same scene repeated all around the barn; new parents with adopted children of all ages, hugging, laughing, crying.

John came up to them, he put his arm round Simeon and said "See what Jesus has done brother? Look how he's changed you? See what affect that change has had on all these people?"

Simeon just nodded, full of emotion from the night's events.

As Simeon and Lydia said goodbye to the last of their guests, Lydia turned to Isaac and Anna, "Right, I think after such a late party, you two need to go to bed."

"But what about clearing up?" asked Isaac, he was still buzzing with excitement and did not feel sleepy at all.

Simeon laughed, "You think you can fool us into thinking you want to clear up? You just want to stay up later! And as your father, I'm telling you to go to bed!"

The children squealed with laughter as Simeon chased them up the stairs to bed.

As he and Lydia tucked them in, the children said, "Goodnight mum and dad" for the first time. It felt so good to all of them.

Life continued relatively peacefully for one more week.

It was early evening, and Simeon had just closed the bakery for the night and was about to go into the kitchen for the evening meal. He had just stepped outside to breathe some fresh air, when Paul, one of his friends, came tearing around the corner carrying a bundle.

"Simeon, take him inside, pray for his arms to grow, say nothing!" and with that, Paul thrust the bundle into Simeon's arms and pushed him through his own door.

Paul shut the door behind him, "Roman soldiers!" he panted, gasping for breath, "Pray for him!"

Simeon was not sure what was going on, but Isaac who was in the kitchen, realised straight away. He took the bundle from Simeon and pulled back the shawl to reveal a small baby, he noticed that he had no arms, just tiny little stumps with a couple of fingers where the arms should have been. He looked at Paul who was still gasping for breath, "They saw you take the baby; they know he has no arms; you want us to pray for his arms to grow so when they get here, they won't know it's the same baby?"

"Yes!" gasped Paul.

"Go out the back way," said Simeon catching on as he pushed Paul into the bakery and out through a back door that was well hidden and not everyone knew was there. When he went back in the kitchen, the children, with Lydia and Leah were all gathered around the baby praying. There was a thump against the door as someone tried to open it!

"Just a moment!" called out Simeon, then he whispered, "Act normally!"

Everyone hastily scurried to sit around the table, except for Lydia who sat in the big chair in the corner holding the baby. Leah began to serve the food.

Simeon opened the door and two Roman soldiers burst in, "Where is he?" they demanded. Anna, Hannah, and Rebekah cowered away from them, they looked angry, and they had big swords.

"Where is who?" asked Simeon.

The soldiers said nothing as they looked around the room. One of the soldiers walked over to the chair where Lydia was holding the baby and roughly pulled open the shawl that was covering him. Anna held her breath. The soldier looked at the baby and covered him up again, "No," he said, shaking his head as he turned back to his fellow soldier. Without another word, they left the house. Simeon shut the door after them.

"Why didn't they take the baby?" asked Anna.

Lydia pulled open the shawl and smiling, held up a perfectly formed little boy! "I suppose they were looking for a baby with no arms!"

Simeon smiled to himself. It seemed ridiculous to him that miracles such as this were happening so often these days that it almost seemed normal!

Paul came back in from the back door, "I heard them go, I stayed by the door."

"What happened, Paul?" asked everyone at once.

"I was with Eli, we saw a man leave the baby and we waited, thinking it was all clear, we couldn't see anyone. I picked the little chap up and saw that he had no arms, so I wrapped him up in the shawl that we had and set off to come here while Eli waited behind. The next thing I knew, Eli was yelling at me to run, and I turned and saw those two soldiers chasing me. I was able to lose them in the alleyways, but they seemed to know where to come!"

"I don't understand," said Isaac, "why chase Paul for taking a baby that they didn't want anyway?" he asked Simeon.

"I don't know," replied Simeon, "I guess they just don't like us interfering with their way of life." He was a little troubled that the Roman soldiers knew where to come, so they decided that from now on, any rescued babies would be taken to different houses, and never the same one twice.

From that time on, Simeon and Lydia noticed an increase in Roman soldiers marching past the bakery.

"I think they're suspicious of us," said Lydia.

"I think you're right, and we know they don't like followers of Jesus," said Simeon.

It was not just the Roman soldiers that seemed to take more of an interest in the bakery. The chief priests had heard that it had become a gathering place for believers and had started to send their temple guards to spy on the bakery.

"A couple of guards came to buy bread today," said Isaac at the dinner table, "It was while you were out getting flour," he looked at Simeon.

"They've been a couple of times now. Did they say anything?" asked Simeon.

"They asked lots of questions about who comes here to visit and why."

"What did you tell them?"

"Well, I wanted to tell them to mind their own business, but I didn't, I just said we have a large family and they come here a lot."

"Well, you're not wrong," smiled Lydia, "we may not have a lot of relatives but if we're talking about God's family, there's a lot of us!"

"That's true," said Simeon looking thoughtful.

Later that night when the children had gone to bed, Simeon, Lydia, and Leah were talking in the kitchen.

"Things are getting worse," said Simeon, "Peter and John were arrested again and flogged, not that that will ever stop them telling people about Jesus and healing the sick! Others have been arrested; some people are leaving Jerusalem. It's not just the chief priests, the Romans seem to hate us too. They've obviously caught wind of something going on here at the bakery. I'm not sure what to do yet, we need to keep the children safe."

Chapter Eighteen

Mary

"You're very quiet this evening," Lydia remarked to Anna as they sat down for dinner.

"What? Oh yeah… sorry, it's just that I saw a lady today when I was out with Isaac, and she reminded me so much of Mary, she looked just like her, I mean, I know it wasn't her, but it was something about the way she walked that made me think of her."

"What was Mary like?" asked Lydia.

"She was really kind, but she didn't stand any nonsense and she protected me from my dad and wasn't afraid of him when he had been drinking. She loved looking after me and cooking for me, but I think she really would have liked to have been able to live with her son and his family. Then she had to send me away so quickly and I miss her and worry about her, and I wish I could tell her I'm safe and she should go and stay with her son and get away from the soldiers in our village." Anna brushed away the tears that were trickling down her cheek.

"Maybe we could visit your village and find her?" suggested Isaac, "It's probably not too far away."

"But I don't know how far it is, or even where it is, I don't even know which city gate we came through!" cried Anna.

"What was your village called?" asked Simeon.

Anna hung her head and said in a whisper, "I don't know. We just called it 'The Village', no one ever called it anything else."

"Well, why don't we ask Jesus to bring her across our path, that somehow we will meet Mary. Maybe she will visit Jerusalem one day. Did she ever come here?" asked Simeon.

"I don't think so, I'm not sure," Anna sighed, "do you think God will answer our prayer? If we ask him to bring Mary to us?"

"I don't see why not!" said Simeon.

So, they prayed together and asked God for the impossible. That he would bring Mary to Jerusalem and that they would find her in a city of thousands!

Years later, when Anna would tell this story, she still marvelled at God's incredible grace and timing that answered her prayer.

Anna was out with Isaac visiting the market, when she caught a glimpse of a girl, of about her own age, who looked vaguely familiar. At first, Anna could not place her, but as she watched the girl choosing some material with her mother, she suddenly realised who she was. She pulled at Isaac's sleeve excitedly, pointing, "Isaac, look! That girl, it's Dara, Mary's granddaughter, I used to play with her when she visited!"

Isaac pulled Anna through the crowded market towards the stall where Dara was with her mother, Rachel, "Come on then, let's get to them before they leave!"

They pushed their way through the crowd and got within earshot, just as Dara and her mother started to walk away from the stall. "Dara!

Rachel!" yelled Anna trying to make herself heard above the noise of the market.

Dara looked round as she heard her name called; her face lit up when she saw Anna. She let go of her mother's hand and ran across to Anna and hugged her.

"What are you doing here?" they both said at the same time.

Rachel, turning to see where her daughter had gone, saw Dara hugging another little girl. As Dara stepped back, Rachel recognised Anna, "Anna! I can't believe my eyes! Is that really you? How?...What?... What on earth are you doing here?"

Anna, ignoring Rachel's question asked, "Is Mary okay? I've missed her so much!"

At that moment, Isaac introduced himself, "Hi, I'm Isaac. Anna's brother."

"I didn't know you had a brother!" said Dara, looking confused.

"Long story, tell me about Mary!"

Rachel answered, "She's fine, worried about you though! She'll be so relieved to know you're safe!"

"I really want to see her, is she still in the village?"

"No, she's actually with us in Jerusalem right now, we're all staying in the city for a few days!" said Rachel.

"Why don't you all come to dinner with us tonight?" asked Isaac, "Our mum and dad would love to meet you."

"Your mum and dad...?" asked Dara looking even more confused.

"Like I said, long story. Good story. Please come, bring everyone. Are Peter and Jotham with you?" Peter was Dara's dad and Jotham her brother.

"Yes, but that would be five of us coming to dinner, don't you think you should check with your...er... parents first?" asked Rachel.

Isaac laughed, "No, mum loves it when we bring people home to eat with us," he still relished being able to say the words 'Mum' and 'home'.

Isaac told them how to find the bakery, and they said goodbye.

Anna gripped Isaac's arm, "Can you believe that! Can you believe that?"

Isaac laughed, "It was only two weeks ago that we asked Jesus to bring Mary to us!"

The children ran home as fast as they could and burst into the bakery where Simeon and Lydia were working.

Anna was out of breath, so they could not quite catch what she was saying at first, so Isaac interrupted, "We found Mary!"

"Your Mary?" asked Lydia of Anna.

Anna nodded, "We didn't actually see her, we met Dara, her grand-daughter, in the market with her mother Rachel. Rachel said Mary's in Jerusalem with them right now, so Isaac invited them all to dinner, there's five of them, is that okay?"

Lydia laughed, "Of course, tell me the whole story, this is wonderful news!" Isaac and Anna told the story, happily interrupting one another.

"So, God has answered our prayers!" laughed Simeon, "I can't wait to meet them all".

Anna was a bundle of nerves and excitement all afternoon in anticipation of seeing Mary.

"Anna, sweetheart, why don't you go outside or into the bakery?" said Lydia as she and Leah began preparing dinner.

"Isaac's clearing up with your dad in the bakery, you could help there?" suggested Leah.

Anna went into the bakery, "They sent me out of the kitchen, I'm not very helpful at the moment," she said to Simeon, "I'm too excited!"

He handed her a broom, "Here, sweep the floor, that will help!"

Anna found it hard to concentrate as she swept up and did not really notice Isaac sweeping behind her getting all the bits she had missed.

ANNA

"Are you sure it was her?" Mary asked her daughter in law again.

"Without a doubt, she looks the same, just better dressed and not as skinny!"

"So, she's been well cared for? How did that happen? And who is this brother you met?" asked Mary again.

"Mum, I've told you all I know! We'll find out very soon."

"I wonder if she'll be the same? We used to have so much fun, do you remember hiding behind that blanket when we played together?" Jotham asked Dara.

Mary shuddered at the memory of Anna hiding behind the blanket all those months ago, terrified. She would feel so much better once she had seen Anna with her own eyes. Mary had not stopped worrying about whether she had done the right thing for Anna; and now she had so much to catch up on!

It would not take them long to walk to the bakery from the inn where they were staying. As they got nearer, Mary began to feel anxious, she wondered how Anna would feel towards her? Had she understood why Mary had sent her away? What had Anna been through? What were the people like that she was staying with?

As the time for Mary's arrival drew near, Anna became more and more excited and was eventually asked by Lydia to go and sit outside on the step to look out for their guests.

After what seemed like an age, Anna spotted Mary and her family walking towards the bakery! She let out a squeal of excitement and ran towards them.

When Mary saw Anna running towards her! She forgot all her worries as Anna flung her arms around Mary's waist laughing with delight.

"Oh, my child!" Mary said over and over, "Let me look at you!"

"Mary!" cried Anna, "Jesus answered our prayer, I so wanted to see you!"

Mary held Anna at arm's length and looked her over. She breathed a sigh of relief as she realised that Anna was clearly happy and healthy, in fact she looked better cared for than she had ever been! Anna said hello to Mary's family and, taking Mary's hand, she dragged her towards the bakery.

Mary looked with amazement at Anna's new home. It appeared to be a large house and bakery with a barn attached.

"Mum, Dad, Isaac! They're here!" Anna called out.

A beaming Simeon came out of the bakery to welcome his guests, "Welcome! Welcome! Come in! Anna's told us all about you!" Simeon invited them inside his home, "I'm Simeon, this is my wife Lydia, this is our son Isaac and our friend Leah and her daughters Hannah and Rebekah."

One by one they said hello as Mary introduced them to her family.

"Anna, how come you ended up here? What happened to you?" asked Mary.

Before Anna could respond, Lydia suggested, "I tell you what, why don't we all sit down and have something to eat then Anna can tell you her story over dinner."

They all sat around the large table. Lydia and Leah served the dinner as Anna began to tell her story. Mary winced when Anna relayed some of the scarier details and Isaac interrupted to give more detail. Mary and her family gasped when Anna told them about the slave traders.

"I should have come with you!" cried Mary, "I don't know why I didn't, I was just worried I would slow you down, or they'd notice if I left as well, and they might have followed..."

"No, Mary, you did the right thing! I can see it now; this was God's plan all along. Everything happened so that I would end up here with my new family!" Anna continued her story and explained how she had ended up with Simeon and Lydia, and how they had rescued many children and babies, and finally, how her and Isaac had been adopted.

Mary had tears in her eyes as she hugged Anna again and said, "Oh Anna, that is some story! Thank goodness you're safe!" Then she turned to Simeon and Lydia, "I can't thank you enough! I've been praying for Jesus to bring Anna across our path and then I was going to offer her a new home, but I can see how God kept her safe and what a wonderful family she has here." Mary turned back to Anna, "I'm so glad for you sweetheart, you look so happy here and I'm so glad you met Jesus and he's changed your family's life!"

"Mary! You know Jesus! How?" asked Anna.

Mary began her own story, "Well, after you left, I had no reason to stay in the village, so I went to live with Peter and his family in Bethany."

"We were really pleased to have Grandma come and live with us!" interrupted Dara.

Mary smiled at her granddaughter, "Yes, it's been wonderful to be with you all. Anyway, there was not really enough room for all of us in the house, so we moved to a bigger house next door to Lazarus and his family who we've got to know quite well. They often talked to us about Jesus; they actually knew him well; he would often visit and share meals with them. One day Lazarus was telling us about the time Jesus raised him from the dead, he had been dead and buried for four days and Jesus brought him back to life! As he was speaking, we found our hearts burning within us and we knew that everything he said to us was true, and we believed in Jesus for ourselves." Mary's family all nodded in confirmation.

Dara chipped in, "We've been asking Jesus to find you ever since we got to know him!"

"Everything I've ever wanted has happened!" laughed Anna as she hugged Mary.

They had some bread and wine together and enjoyed the sense of Jesus' presence being with them.

It was getting late when Mary and her family left with promises all round that they would meet up again soon.

After they had gone, Anna climbed onto Simeon's lap, "I'm the happiest person in the world!" she cried as Simeon hugged her.

Isaac and Lydia, and Leah with Hannah and Rebekah all came and joined in the hug as they laughed together.

On the one hand, life was good! Babies and children were rescued and adopted by believers who were more than happy to give these orphans a home. Families were helped who were so desperately poor, given food to eat and somewhere to sleep if they needed it. The story of this new life through Jesus was shared with everyone who met Simeon's family, and many believed and were baptised. Every day, across Jerusalem, more and more people believed in Jesus as people were healed and changed by him.

On the other hand, as word spread amongst the poor and needy that the bakery was a place of refuge, and a place to get to know Jesus, so word had also reached the ears of the chief priests that the bakery was an influential gathering place for the followers of Jesus. Many people were becoming believers as a direct result of what Simeon and Lydia were doing and the religious authorities were greatly disturbed by the rumours they were hearing. The chief priests and religious leaders enjoyed their status, enjoyed lording it over people and were full of pride and considered themselves special because of their position in the community. They had been continuing to arrest the disciples of Jesus, flogging, and threatening them, but the news about Jesus was still spreading and now, with so many people following Jesus and his disciples, they were losing their influence and power over the people.

Something had to be done.

But they had to be cautious, they did not want to start a riot by openly arresting Simeon just for doing good.

The answer for the chief priests came in the form of a man named Saul. He was a devout Jew, learned and very zealous for their religion. He would find the 'evidence' they needed to stop these troublemakers!

Chapter Nineteen

Escape

Anna and Isaac wandered back into the bakery feeling a little weary and downcast, it had been some time now since they had found anyone who needed their help. The barn that was sometimes full of children and families, was empty, apart from Leah and her girls.

"But it's good really!" said Isaac, "What if there is no-one else to be rescued?"

"There must be!" replied Anna, "What if we're missing them?"

"Remember what dad always says, 'You can trust God!' so we don't need to worry!" reassured Isaac.

As they walked in, the atmosphere in the house was tense, which these days was unusual. Andrew and Naomi were there looking pale and bewildered.

Alarmed, Isaac and Anna immediately asked what was wrong.

Simeon walked over to them and put his big strong arms around them; he wanted to protect the children from what he had just heard but knew by the look on their faces that he could not hide it from them.

"Come and sit down," he said.

Isaac and Anna did so, feeling a sense of dread. Lydia came and sat on the other side of them.

"We've just heard some sad news. A man named Stephen, who was a believer, has died," said Simeon.

"How did he die?" asked Anna.

"What happened to him? Was he ill? Why didn't Jesus heal him?" asked Isaac.

Simeon sighed, "I don't know why God allows some things to happen, all I know is that I trust him. Stephen has been stoned to death by the religious authorities, they charged him with blasphemy because a man named Saul paid wicked men to lie about him. Apparently, Saul is doing this more and more to believers all over the city, he seems to have been given authority to have believers in Jesus killed or imprisoned."

"That's terrible!" cried Isaac, "Why didn't Jesus rescue him?"

"Jesus did warn us that we would have trouble and be persecuted, but apparently, as Stephen was being stoned, his face shone, and he said he could see Jesus. So, although it's sad, it's also a great comfort to know that he's with Jesus now."

"But what if this man Saul comes after us?" worried Anna.

"Anna, I will do my best to keep you safe, but he won't come after you and Isaac, you're children," said Simeon.

"But what about you and Lydia?" asked Isaac.

Simeon did not answer, he did not know how to comfort or reassure Isaac. All they could do was pray together and ask God for wisdom and put their trust in Jesus.

A few nights later, Isaac and Anna could not get to sleep, "I just feel like things are changing," worried Anna.

"Me too," replied Isaac, "but at least we're not on our own this time!"

Downstairs, Simeon and Lydia were gathering together some of their most treasured possessions including some money that they had not put with the bankers.

They held one another for a while, "We may not have to leave," Simeon tried to reassure Lydia.

They had not told the children all that had been going on over the last few days since Stephen had died. A growing persecution had broken out against the followers of Jesus, fuelled by the chief priests and their new friend Saul. People had been dragged out of their homes and thrown into prison; more and more believers were fleeing Jerusalem.

"Simeon, it's only a matter of time before they come for us. If it weren't for the children I'd be tempted to stay, but I can't bear the thought of them becoming orphans again!" said Lydia.

At that moment, Leah came into the kitchen, "Hannah and Rebekah are asleep, and I've packed a few essentials." she said.

"We don't know if or when to go," explained Simeon, "let's just pray together, I need to know what the Holy Spirit wants us to do".

As the three of them were praying, there was an urgent knock on the door. Simeon answered cautiously as Lydia and Leah anxiously looked on.

It was John. He hurried through the door and said, "You need to leave Jerusalem now! Right this minute. Saul and his temple guards are on their way to your house."

"How do you...?" began Simeon.

"Doesn't matter! Just get the children and go, trust me!" interrupted John.

Isaac and Anna had heard everything; having still been awake, they had crept downstairs when they heard John arrive and were listening quietly. They burst into the kitchen.

"Get your sandals and cloaks on quickly!" urged Lydia.

Leah had already woken Hannah and Rebekah who were stumbling into the kitchen bleary eyed and confused. Isaac and Anna quickly grabbed their cloaks and put their sandals on as fast as they could, Isaac had to help Anna because she was panicking a bit and could not tie her sandals.

Back in the kitchen, John carefully opened the door and peeked outside to see if it was safe to leave, "I can see Saul's men, they're close! Do you have another way out? We need to get to David and Esther's."

"Yes, through the bakery, there's a door out the back," said Isaac.

He led the way, Simeon grabbing Anna's hand and Lydia and Leah holding tightly onto Hannah and Rebekah who was now crying.

"Hush Rebekah," comforted Leah, "it will be okay".

The family, along with John, hurried out through the back of the bakery and closed the door. Within a few moments, they heard the front door of their house being forced open. They did not stop to listen, they ran, following Isaac who knew the streets better than anyone.

Up ahead, they saw David open his door and beckon them in frantically. David and his wife Esther had stayed in the barn for a few weeks when times were hard, so they knew them quite well.

They crammed into the small house, "Quick, down here!" David whispered, as he opened a trapdoor in the floor that had been concealed by a rug.

The large family climbed down some steps into a cellar - which brought back some rather unpleasant memories for Anna and Isaac. It was small and cramped and only the children could stand upright in it, except for Isaac who was now as tall as Lydia. They sat down on the floor of the cellar, "I can hear them going into other people's houses, they will probably come here in a moment, so keep quiet." instructed David.

David shut the trapdoor, put the rug back over it and sat down with his wife.

"Everyone stay completely still and quiet!" urged Simeon as he pulled a terrified Anna onto his lap. She buried her face in his chest hardly daring to breathe.

There was a sharp intake of breath from all of them when they heard the temple guards barge their way into David's house, "What do you want? What are you doing in my house?" they heard David demand.

"We're looking for Simeon the baker, he and his family are wanted for questioning," said Saul as he walked in after his guards.

"Well, as you can see, the only people in this room are me and my wife!" said David.

Isaac looked up at the ceiling of their refuge, seeing nothing, but hearing the temple guards walking around the small house. It did not take long.

"Let's go!" Saul said to his men, and turning to David he threatened, "If I find out you know anything about this, I'll be back!"

Saul and his guards left, and everyone in the cellar breathed a sigh of relief. David whispered through a gap in the floorboards of the trapdoor, "Stay there for a bit until I know for sure that they're gone!"

It was half an hour later that David opened the trapdoor and let everyone out.

"Sorry, it took a while, they were searching nearby houses. I think it's safe now, but we'd better keep quiet," said David.

"Thank you, David, and you Esther for rescuing us!" said Simeon.

David laughed quietly and patted him on the shoulder, "Well you rescued us a few months ago!"

"What now?" asked Leah, her arms around Hannah and Rebekah.

"You need to leave the city before dawn," said John.

"But all the gates will be closed this late at night!" said Isaac.

"True," replied John, "but I have a way out, and I'll take you there."

David opened the door and checked outside, "It's clear!"

They said hurried goodbyes and followed John. They went down many winding streets and passageways until they came close to the edge of the city and the large wall that surrounded Jerusalem. Isaac and Anna did not dare make a noise, constantly looking around for Saul and his men.

John quietly knocked on the door of a very ordinary looking house. He had to knock a few times to wake the man inside.

"John, what is it? Oh...." he exclaimed as he saw the extra seven people with John.

He opened his door wide and invited them in, "You don't need to explain," he grimaced, "I heard that Saul was hunting down believers. You're not the first to come my way. Follow me."

He led them to the back of the room, and with John's help, moved a large dresser to one side to reveal a wooden door.

"This is where we go our separate ways," said John, "I'm staying in Jerusalem, but I know it's God's will for you to go. We will meet again my brother," he said as he embraced Simeon with tears in his eyes. He pointed towards the wooden door, "Behind that door is a passageway out of the city, it runs under the wall. You won't be seen by anyone, but there are a lot of steps to climb once you've gone under the wall, and you'll come out in an olive grove just up the hill. Go quickly now, stay safe and may our Lord bless you and keep you."

The man - whose name they did not know - lit a torch and handed it to them. He opened the door and gently guided them through. Simeon barely had time to thank his new friend before the door was closed behind them and they were on their own. Simeon held the torch up ahead of him to show a narrow passageway winding downwards.

"Is everyone okay?" he whispered, as he turned around to see their pale faces.

They all nodded; no-one said a word as they were all in shock at the speed of their exodus from Jerusalem.

"Follow me, it will be okay," he reassured them.

The passageway went steeply downwards for a while, then flat for even longer, until they came to the steps. John was right, there were a lot of steps to climb! It was not easy as they were steep and uneven.

Eventually as they drew near to the top of the steps, a small breeze made the flame of the torch flicker. Simeon extinguished the light, and they began to see the moonlit sky through a gap in the rocks ahead. They found themselves stepping out into a dense olive grove up on the hillside above Jerusalem. "Let's sit down to rest for a moment," said Simeon panting.

They sat silently and gazed back at Jerusalem below them, "Will we ever come back?" asked Lydia.

"I don't know love."

"Everything you've built is there, your bakery, the barn" she trailed off.

"But everyone I love is here," he said as he looked at his extended family.

After a short rest, they set off to find somewhere to spend the rest of the night. "Don't worry!" said Isaac, "This is where I come in, I know how to find the best places to sleep. Follow me!"

He found an old stone shelter that was used by goatherds but was currently empty. Simeon had been carrying Rebekah who was already asleep. They settled down gratefully on the sheltered ground and one by one fell asleep.

The next morning, Simeon was the first to wake and he gently shook everyone else awake.

He handed round the goatskin full of water and took some bread out of his bag for everyone to eat.

"Where do we go now?" asked Anna.

"I'm not sure," replied Simeon, "all I am certain about is that we can't go back. But listen, I know this is a first for some of us, but God will show us the way and provide everything we need. Lydia and I have always had more than enough money, even after we gave most of it away, the bakery was so successful that we always had plenty for ourselves and all the other families that we fed. But now, for the first time, we are truly dependant on Jesus to look after us and feed us."

"I trust you, Simeon," said Leah, "I wouldn't be here without you and Lydia, and I'm up for our next adventure!"

All the children agreed, "So are we!"

As they set off, Anna walked just a little way behind and watched her family. She watched Isaac; taller, stronger, and more confident than ever, growing into a man. Leah; looking younger and happier than she had ever seen her. Hannah and Rebekah holding hands chatting away, no longer timid and fearful. And finally, she looked at Simeon and Lydia, her new mum and dad, who, despite their current circumstances, were more peaceful and contented than they had ever been.

Even though she was walking into the unknown, Anna felt safe. Every one of their lives had been changed and enriched by Jesus and she knew she was not alone, she was a beloved daughter, not just of Simeon and Lydia, but of God himself.

www.ingramcontent.com/pod-product-compliance
Lightning Source LLC
Chambersburg PA
CBHW050528260626
47157CB00004B/1514